A Time
To Lie

By D.W. HARDIN

ISBN-13: 978-0-9849179-1-4

ACKNOWLEDGEMENTS

As usual, there are so many people who have helped me that I don't know where to begin. It is almost mind boggling when I think of how many people gave up their time helping. I wish to thank all of the following. Lt. Joseph Lannan and Deputy Randal Hogan for giving technical advice helping me avoid mistakes. I wish to thank Major Gerald Bates, Captain Michael James, Officer Joseph Castellano and Sgt. Jerry Bolton for their assistance. I am fortunate to have two ladies, Carmen Hardin and Thelma Haley, who tirelessly edit and re-edit my work. I thank Sheriff John Aubrey for allowing me to be part of a truly professional law enforcement agency.

CONTENTS

PROLOGUE

The sidewalk became crowded with a crush of people. It was as if people appeared out of nowhere surrounding the two men. A drama was unfolding before their eyes without a purchase price attached. A few became ill and turned away. Others pushed closer not to miss anything. Two burly bouncers from the bar fronting the scene were losing the battle to keep the spectators back. Light reflected off the bouncers' shaven heads from the bar's neon lights.

A man was propped against the rear wheel of a Cadillac Escalade which had seen its better days. A second man, considerably younger than the first, was feverishly trying to stay the flow of blood from the upper thigh of the other man. The young man had blood splatters all over him. His arms were covered with red up to the elbows. A large artery had been severed, and he was unsuccessfully trying to stop the flow. Life was seeping out with each heart beat.

A second crowd had gathered about fifteen feet further down the sidewalk. A circle had formed around a body lying prone on the sidewalk. A black hoodie obscured part of the face. There was one hole in the back. A dark wet stain was enlarging around the hole. Underneath the body, a sanguineous pool seeped across the concrete towards the gutter. The body was still. Death had taken possession.

The shrill wail of sirens pierced the darkness from several directions as police, EMTs and firefighters responded. Two marked police cars arrived almost simultaneously with an ambulance arriving seconds behind.

The flashing blue and red emergency lights gave the scene a surreal appearance making people appear to move in jerky movements. Two men in dark blue uniforms with holstered weapons pushed their way through the crowd. One glance told the police officers the story. There had been a shooting.

CHAPTER 1

I found myself in the back of a homicide detective's Crown Vic heading to headquarters to give a statement of what happened tonight. There's not much leg room in the backseat of a Crown Vic with a prisoner cage. I didn't know if homicide or internal affairs would be doing the investigation. I figured it would be IA being I was a cop. I was wrong. I wish I had not taken this off duty job, but Frank, a fellow cop, talked me into it. He said he needed a second officer; otherwise, the job would fall through. I really didn't want the job, but I needed the money. Frank said the job paid thirty dollars an hour, cash. Cash I wouldn't have to report as income.

My wife, Sarah, and I have been separated for two months. I let her keep the house because I still cared for Sarah, and we had a toddler named Amy. I didn't want Sarah or my daughter living in some low rent apartment. Sarah is a part time paralegal at a law firm. We had agreed she needed to be home with Amy as much as possible. She barely makes enough to pay for childcare much less pay rent and provide groceries.

I ended up making the mortgage payment and giving her a little money for food. It didn't leave much for me. I'm living in a second rate apartment getting half my rent free because I'm a cop. It's a quid quo pro deal. If there's trouble, the management calls me. I've been lucky so far. I've only had to chase off a few loitering teens.

I knew Frank liked the ladies from the gossip in the locker room. Cops gossip more than old ladies. But I never knew how much Frank liked the ladies. He was all over one of the bar girls named Brandy – if it was really her name. It was lingerie night at the bar. Brandy wore a thin dark red chemise with a very revealing black bra and matching bikini panties. He had his hands on her all night. Of course, she didn't seem to mind the attention. She'd rub against him making sure the appropriate parts made contact.

Brandy was about five foot four. She was fighting the few extra pounds that middle age brings to sometimes. I guessed she was somewhere between 35 to 38 years old. The dark roots of her hair shouted she wasn't a natural blond. At one time, she must have been a handsome woman, but her lifestyle had taken its toll. I wondered how much longer her body would allow this occupation. Youth has a way of pushing the old out of the way. What would she do when the game ended? I'd never know the answer. I didn't need to know.

I didn't consider Frank a handsome man. He hadn't taken care of his body. His stomach hung over his belt. Frank's face was a permanent ruddy red from too much alcohol. I considered his language crude. Many of his remarks around the bar girls had sexual overtones. I'd already decided I wouldn't work with Frank again. Hind sight is always 20/20.

Frank probably spent everything he made that night buying Brandy overpriced drinks. Frank knew the drinks were mostly water, and she'd get her cut of the take. During her "break", Frank disappeared with her to the parking lot which wasn't well lighted. I didn't go out to see what they were doing. It was none of my business. Besides, a lot of the girls disappeared with customers for a short time. I turned a blind eye to the activity. It was a "don't ask, don't tell" situation. We were making top dollar for this gig.

When Frank returned with the girl, he waved for me to come to the front door. I wasn't wearing a jacket, just a pullover shirt to conceal my weapon. The season was changing, and Mother Nature hadn't made up her mind whether it would be warm or cold. It was crisp in the morning and warm in the afternoon with night extending its realm over day.

I knew what he wanted. He wanted me to keep my mouth shut about his activities tonight. It was fine by me as long as I got paid. I could truthfully say I saw nothing. I followed him out the front door onto the sideway when I heard him scream, "Gun!"

Frank was drawing his weapon. He blocked my view so I stepped to his right while drawing my pistol. I heard a shot, but it sounded like it

4

came from behind me. Frank fell to the sidewalk yelling he was hit and holding his thigh with both hands. A man in a black hoodie and jeans was standing fifteen feet in front of us holding a revolver at a forty-five degree angle with a surprised expression on his face.

A second man, dressed in a dark sweatshirt, baggy blue jeans and jogging shoes was sprinting away from the scene. He didn't look back as he sprinted into an alley. Everything seemed to be moving in slow motion. I think I identified myself as a police officer, but I'm not sure. It happened so fast.

I was in a Weaver's stance. I fired twice -- double tap to center mass just like we're trained. The man fell forward dropping the revolver. I quickly walked to the suspect taking my foot to rake the weapon out of his reach. He wasn't moving. I felt the side of his neck with my index finger. There was no pulse.

I holstered my pistol and ran to Frank. He had dragged himself into a sitting position leaning against the rear tire of a burgundy Cadillac. Blood was squirting in the air from the leg wound. It flashed into my mind we were told in training that most officers bled out when shot in the thigh because the femoral artery was usually hit. Frank's face was chalky white. I applied pressure on the wound. It didn't work.

I unhitched my belt sliding my weapon and my badge off the belt, laying them next to me. Looping the belt around where the thigh joins the hip, I cinched the belt as tight as I could. Nothing helped. Bright red blood ebbed from the wound. I remember hands pulling me away from Frank as EMT's took my place. A man in civilian clothes with a weapon and badge on his right hip had picked up my pistol. He had on vinyl gloves. He removed the magazine and uncharged the weapon before dropping all of it into a paper bag. I knew what the bag was – an evidence bag. A second man, whom I recognized as a homicide detective, took me by the arm and said, "Let's get you out of here. I'll take you to headquarters. You can give your statement there."

***

The ride to headquarters was a blur. I remember the heavy radio traffic as units called in blocking streets for the ambulance to get Frank to the hospital. When an officer is injured, we take care of our own. There

5

would be police escorts clearing the way for the ambulance. The detective was silent for the whole drive. It didn't matter. I was in a fog, perhaps shock. I thought about the instructors at the academy discussing police shootings. The instructors stated that an officer usually didn't remember how many times the trigger had been pulled when involved in a shooting. When asked, the officer would state he had discharged his weapon once or twice whereas he had actually shot eight or more times. He wasn't lying. That's what he actually remembered.

I knew they were going to grill me. I would be treated like a suspect until cleared. I tried to recall what I was taught about interrogation techniques. A suspect's body language is important. Often, detectives decided whether a suspect's testimony was truthful or fraudulent by body language. If they decided the suspect was lying, they'd keep probing until the suspect cracked, telling the truth, or requesting a lawyer. Once a suspect asked for a lawyer, all questioning ceased.

I had to look the questioner in the eyes. If you won't make eye contact, there's something you're not telling. Keep my hands calmly resting on the table and don't fidget. It makes you look guilty. Don't look at the ceiling. Guilty people buy time to fabricate a story by looking upwards. Only answer the questions asked. Don't volunteer any information. It could be used to box you into a trap. Most importantly, stick your story. If you change one little part of it, then the whole story is questionable.

***

I was led to one of the small interrogation rooms. There were no amenities in the room, a concrete block cell with one way in and one way out. A metal table and uncomfortable chair were secured to the floor in the far corner. There was a movable chair on the opposite side of the table for the interrogator. If a second detective was present, he'd bring a chair with him. The room was brilliantly lighted. I knew they'd be taping the whole session. Afterwards, they'd review the tape and decide my fate.

They let me sit in the room with the door closed. I knew what they were doing. They were letting me sweat. All the time they were watching me on a monitor. Cops are hard to interrogate. We know their techniques. I slumped in the chair closing my eyes. I felt large beads of sweat running down my temples. I hoped they didn't pick it up on the camera. It seemed like an eternity before the door opened. I heard the door latch but decided not to open my eyes. Let them be the first to speak.

I heard a man clearing his throat and a chair scraping on the floor. I opened my eyes remaining silent. A man I guessed to be in his late forties was sitting facing me. He was dressed in a long sleeved white shirt with the sleeves rolled to the elbows. The dark blue tie was wrinkled with a damp stain like he had tried to clean it. The pants were off the rack from some bargain store along with well worn low cut black shoes. The close cropped haircut accentuated his balding. He was a rather nondescript man which was good for a detective.

On the table in front of him was a yellow legal tablet with a file folder underneath it. The tablet had some writing on it. He flipped the page over when he saw me trying to read it. Cops are curious. It's in our makeup. He had a Styrofoam cup of black coffee beside the tablet. He hadn't brought me any coffee. This wasn't going to be a friendly interrogation. We locked eyes. It was going to be a test of wills. Cops are strong willed.

He spoke first, "Officer Drake, I'm Captain Searcy, Homicide. You have the same constitutional rights accorded to any citizen. In other words, Miranda applies to you. If at any time you want to stop the interview, you may do so.

I nodded my head affirmatively. Searcy said, "As you know, this session is being taped. You will have to verbally answer."

"Yes," I answered.

"Let me clarify the question with a few points so that there is no misunderstanding," stated Searcy keeping eye contact. "At the present, this is a homicide investigation. It is not an internal affairs investigation. Internal affairs will receive our report and will decide if they need to be involved. It is departmental policy to place you on administrative leave with pay. You will receive a written letter within twenty-four hours explaining. Your police powers are suspended until the matter is cleared. You will be required to submit a written report. That's departmental policy. Do you understand everything I have explained?"

I answered, "Yes."

Searcy then read me the Miranda warning. Fear twisted my guts. Searcy was a play by the book son of a bitch. He was carefully laying out the rules. If I fucked up, he'd pounce on me. There'll be no give and take.

7

He was a predator. I started to tell him I wanted an attorney. The FOP would pay the bill, but it would make me look like I did something wrong. I simply answered, "I understand."

***

Thankfully I had driven my personal car; otherwise, I'd be walking. I couldn't drive my take home unit with my police powers suspended. On the drive home, the interview replayed over and over in my head like a recording in a loop. I felt like I had a touch of OCD. It had not gone well. A headache was starting in the back of my skull. I assume it was a tension headache. God knows I've been under a lot of stress.

I tried to push the interview out of my mind, but it wouldn't go away. The captain asked me to state my name, rank, badge number, assignment and length of time on the force. He had all the information, but he wanted it in the transcript. He stated I'd get an opportunity to review the transcript for mistakes.

I answered, "John Drake, patrolman, badge 466, third district on second shift. Five years."

Then he had me tell what happened. I couldn't read anything from his facial features as I relived the nightmare. I was finishing when he was called out of the office. Returning, his body language was different. He was colder if that was possible. Searcy didn't speak for a moment. He sat tapping his pen on the table as if he were making up his mind about something. Giving me a hard stare, he said, "The officer didn't make it. He died at the hospital. The homicide detective at the hospital said the doctors stated it was a large caliber gunshot wound. The exit wound was in the front of the leg. He was shot from behind. The man you shot had a .22 caliber revolver. He hadn't fired any rounds."

I was dumbfounded. I'm sure he saw the puzzled expression on my face. I knew I had heard a shot, and it wasn't a small caliber. A .22 doesn't make the loud discharge I heard. Cocking his head as if in thought, Searcy asked, "Could you have heard a car backfiring or something else?"

I didn't know if he was trying to give me a way out of the box or closing the lid. I wasn't taking any chances. I stuck to my story, "No, it was definitely a large caliber weapon. I know the difference between a car backfiring and a large caliber gun. It was a gun."

8

I pulled the car to the curb because I couldn't concentrate on driving. It felt like an axe had been buried in my forehead. Doubt crept into my mind. Could there have been a car I hadn't seen? I had tunnel vision that most cops get when focused on a dangerous situation. I lost awareness of my surrounding strictly concentrating on the threat. I couldn't recall any cars passing in close proximity when Frank and I walked out the front door. A car would have been next to us for a backfire to be so loud. I couldn't have missed that. Could I?

I know I fired only two rounds. Shit, I couldn't check the magazine to see how many rounds were left. Homicide had my pistol. I was carrying my duty pistol, a Glock .40 caliber model 35. It carried fifteen rounds. Searcy knew how many rounds were left. Was he telling me I had shot more than two times? Or, was he playing with me? Was he trying to catch me in a lie? Of course, I could have charged the pistol and slipped another round in the magazine. It was against policy, but a lot of cops did it. The spent shell casings should be on the sidewalk unless a spectator picked one up as a souvenir. People do stupid things. That's why crime scenes are roped off.

***

I pulled next to my marked unit in my apartment's lot having convinced myself that I had killed Frank. Damn, I had killed two men tonight. Had I killed two innocent men? Was the man with the revolver lowering it or raising it? A visual image of one of the instructors at the academy flashed into my mind. I vividly recalled him standing in front of the recruit class saying, "There will be situations requiring you to make a decision in less than a second.

"The decision will be irreversible. It may be of such magnitude it will affect whether you stay in law enforcement or seek another field. You will not have the opportunity to think. You will unconsciously fallback on your training. It's called muscle memory. After making a physical movement multiple times, the brain replicates the action without conscious thought."

I was still thinking about what the instructor had said as I unlocked my apartment's door. The phone was ringing. I closed the door behind me without bothering to lock it and walked to the phone. The caller ID showed it was my father calling. I didn't want to talk with him. I'm sure he had seen the shooting on the news or somebody had called him. He had not been happy with my career choice.

I really don't know what happened, but Dad and I had grown apart since I became a police officer. At every family gathering he always brought up I could be earning a lot more money in a different field with my college degree without the danger involved in being a cop. He couldn't comprehend I liked being a cop.

After the phone stopped ringing, I thumbed the caller ID to see who else had called. Sarah had called. God, I miss her. I started to call her but decided against it. I was afraid we'd end up in an argument. It seemed that all we ever did was fight. It wasn't like that when we first married. When Amy was born, money became tight. I worked all the overtime I could get. I didn't see much of my family because I was always working or sleeping.

She said I had changed. I had become cynical and suspicious of people. What did she expect? I dealt with lying assholes every day. I stopped talking about the job. She didn't understand. It has been estimated the divorce rate for cops runs as high as seventy-five percent. I was on my way to being part of that statistic. I wish there was some way we could get back together.

There were a couple of hard bangs on the door. It swung open with my sergeant filling the doorway. He had his fist raised as if he were going to hammer the door again. Shaking his head, he said, "You've got to learn to lock your door."

I didn't want to talk, but I couldn't see any way of turning him away. I waved him into the apartment as I turned to walk to the kitchen. I picked up two glasses out of the sink. The few glasses I have were in need of cleaning. I rinsed them out drying only the outside. I didn't have any ice so I poured an inch of Evan William's whiskey into the glasses. Leaning against the counter, I handed one to him. He tossed the whiskey back in one gulp refilling his glass while I sipped mine. As he was pouring, he said, "You didn't answer your phone. I was concerned and decided to come by to see if you were OK."

The sarge was a veteran on the force with twenty plus years under his belt. His ebony skin was a shade lighter than the dark blue uniform he wore. He was a big man without an ounce of fat on his frame. His bald head gleamed as if he had waxed it. His uniform looked like it had been freshly laundered although I knew he had worn it all day.

The sarge could have been higher in rank, but he chose not to take the promotion tests. When questioned, he stated that he wasn't totally willing to leave the action on the street. He became a sergeant because he couldn't keep up with the young pups. It was a vicarious arrangement.

After blowing out a deep breath, he said, "I needed that. Listen, I came by to give some advice. Get yourself a good lawyer. You're going to need one."

"The Fraternal Order of Police will provide one. I'll call in the morning," I answered.

"No, you're going to need a top of the line attorney," he stated shaking his head like a father speaking to a young son. "Not that crap attorney the FOP uses. Somebody like Henry Fellows."

"Shit, I can't afford Fellows. He'll throw me out of his office," I scoffed.

"You can't afford not to have somebody like him. The word's already on the street that you screwed up! The press will be all over this. They'll try you before the facts are in. The street cops will stand by you, but the brass's another matter. They'll be like dogs stiffing the air to see which way the scent is blowing. If it smells bad, they'll throw you under the bus."

Scratching his head as if trying to remember, the sarge said, "I know you've given a statement, but you'll be called back to clarify some points as the investigation progresses. If you're not sure of a fact, tell them that you don't know. Don't give them a chance to go on a fishing expedition with suppositions."

"That could be construed as lying," I argued.

"Damnit, then it's a time to lie!" he snapped back at me. "It's your neck stretched on the chopping block. Don't hand them the axe."

We stood there staring at each other. I knew he was speaking from experience. I was in trouble.

CHAPTER 2

I couldn't sleep last night. Earlier in the evening, the phone was the problem. It kept ringing. I didn't recognize many of the numbers on the caller ID. How did they get my phone number? Like most cops, I had an unlisted number, but I know there's ways of getting it. There was one caller I sure as hell wasn't going to have any communication with. Our local newspaper's name kept coming up on the caller ID.

The reporter who was calling was persistent – must have called every twenty minutes. The reporter probably got my number from a cop. Finally, I unplugged the phone and tried to sleep. The shooting was like a video tape in a loop constantly replaying in my head. The nightmare changed as it replayed. I lay in bed covered with sweat staring at the ceiling hearing Frank ask, "Why'd you kill me John?"

I could feel the bile rising in my throat as I sprang out of bed running to the bathroom. I was on my knees hugging the toilet bowl with my face inches above the water dry heaving. I thought about dunking my head into the water and drowning myself. Pushing myself away from the bowl, I sat against the bathroom wall in the darkness crying. I don't know if I was crying for myself or for Frank. I hadn't cried like this since I was a small child. Snot streamed from my nose as I cried out in primordial anguish as if my soul was wounded.

I didn't feel like eating so I decided to make some coffee. As it was brewing, I left the apartment, walked to the corner and dropped fifty cents into a newspaper machine. It was too dark for me to read so I tucked it under my arm walking back to my apartment. The aromatic smell of coffee greeted me as I entered. I flipped the newspaper on the small scarred kitchen table. Then I rinsed a mug filling it with the black syrup. I like my coffee black and strong.

Sitting at the table, I saw I made the headlines. It read TWO SHOOTING DEATHS AT NIGHTCLUB. My whole body felt on fire as nerves went out of control. I think my blood pressure skyrocketed off the chart. I didn't want the coffee anymore. I was shaking so hard I spilled it as I set the mug on the table. The reporter had carefully worded the story. Using un-named sources, he stated there was an investigation as to how the dead officer was killed. It was apparent he had a cop leaking information. This was going to get nasty real quick.

I needed to do something to settle my nerves. Usually, when I'm stressed out, I go to the gym for a hard work out with weights. I didn't want to go because I knew there'd be other cops there. I didn't want to answer any questions. As I said before, cops are curious. Leaving everything on the table, I slipped on a tee shirt and jogging shorts. As I laced up my shoes, I decided I'd call the attorney, Henry Fellows, after a hard run.

* * *

The phone was answered on the second ring. A pleasant woman's voice stated, "Henry Fellows attorney at law. How may I help you?"

"I'm John Drake," I answered. "I need an appointment with Mr. Fellows as soon as possible."

There was a perceptible pause before she answered, "Would you please hold for a moment?"

Odds were she recognized my name from reading the newspaper. An older man's voice came on line, "Mr. Drake, this is Henry Fellows. I don't wish to speak over the telephone. Could you be at my office by eleven today?"

"Yes sir," I answered.

"Fine, I'll see you at eleven," he stated. The line went dead.

As I put the phone down, I heard a soft knocking on the door. I peered through the door's peephole seeing a woman I didn't expect. I opened the door to face my estranged wife, Sarah. Although her eyes were puffy from crying, she looked beautiful to me. At five foot six, a hundred twenty pounds, Sarah had a natural athletic build with a slender compact frame. She kept her blonde hair in a short page cut accentuating her cobalt blue eyes. She was simply dressed in jeans with a white sweatshirt and tennis shoes.

Physically, she was the complete opposite of me. At five foot eleven and one hundred eighty-five pounds, I'd be described as stout. I keep my coal black hair short for occupational reasons. People can't hold onto your hair if it's short. Sarah preferred me to wear my hair longer. She said it had a blue sheen when I was in the sunlight. My brown eyes were so dark they almost appeared black.

Reaching to touch my arm, she said, "I rang the doorbell several times. I don't know how long I've been standing outside. I was about to give up."

My eyes misted as I took her hand leading her into the unkempt apartment. Sarah's eyes roved around, but she made no comment. Releasing her hand, I said, "I should have called."

"Yes, you should have," she answered, but there was no hint of reproach in her voice. "Your father called me. I called last night, but I didn't know if you'd be home. Your mother's watching Amy. I came as soon as I could."

I couldn't stop the tears as I choked out the words, "Sarah, I've missed you so much…"

The conversation ended as she buried her face into my chest. We both stood there crying. Between sobs, she said, "We took vows… We both made mistakes… I have to own my part."

Between sobs, I said, "I'll make it right with you. I promise."

She backed away from me wiping tears from her cheeks looking up at me. Her small cupid lips were turning up in the corners forming the smile that I always loved, "Come home with me. We'll work it out."

Those few simple words were a catharsis. I'd been given a second chance. I wasn't going to blow it. No more holding back about the job, "I think I'm in trouble, Sarah. I have an appointment with a lawyer this morning. I'll tell you everything when I get home, but I don't want to talk to anybody else."

"We've got a problem," she stated. I notice she said "we". "There's a reporter with another man, probably a camera man, parked next to your police car."

"How do you know it's a reporter?" I asked.

"The car has channel 12 on its side. He's planning to ambush you when you go to your car. It'd look bad if you refused to talk to him. That's probably what he's hoping. It'd make a good news clip."

"Crap!" was my single word response.

"He thinks he's got you," she said with a frown pausing to think. "He doesn't know that I'm your wife. The apartment hallway has a back entrance. You come out the back, and I'll pick you up in my car. Duck down in the seat. He'll never know you left. Hope he stays there all day wasting his time."

***

Henry Fellows' office was in the high rent district in the center of downtown. I knew what the sarge had said, but I had serious doubts whether I could afford Fellows' services. The elevator to the eighteenth floor had mirrored walls. I couldn't help but study my reflection. I was dressed in a blue blazer, a regimental striped tie, dark grey slacks and black loafers. The blazer was the only dress coat I had. Seems I was always dressed in blue. That part of my life, I could and would change.

In the reception area, an older woman sat at a desk behind a dark walnut banister using a computer. She was in her late forties with platinum blonde hair and grey eyes. Cops take in details. It's part of our training. She smiled asking, "May I help you?"

"I'm John Drake. I have an appointment with Mr. Fellows."

"He's expecting you. Please follow me." I followed her to a wide hallway which had several closed doors. I noted none of the doors had name plates. I wondered if other attorneys were behind the closed doors. She went to the last office entering without knocking and motioned me in.

A slender man that I guessed to be about the same age as my sergeant sat behind a mammoth cherry desk reading today's paper. I judged him to be approximately my height. His brown hair was graying at the temples. He wore a charcoal pinstripe suit especially cut for his body. An inch of French cuffs were exposed under the coat's sleeves. The silk blue tie was set off by the white shirt which looked imported. Everything about him said expensive.

He studied me for a moment, "Mr. Drake, I assume? Margret, would you please get Mr. Drake and me some coffee? Oh, and hold my calls. I don't want to be disturbed."

Margret left without comment closing the heavy door behind her. Fellows folded the newspaper placing it on the desk with the headline facing me. I wondered if it was done purposefully. "Margret's been with me since I started practicing law. I think she knows more about the law than I do," he quipped with the beginnings of a smile. "Margret brought me the newspaper with the article about the incident. Obviously, I know you have concerns, but what do you think I can do for you?"

He was direct. I had to say that about him. I wondered if I had made a mistake coming to him. To me, it sounded like he wasn't interested or didn't want my case. Perhaps he thought I couldn't afford him. I answered in a stammering voice, "My sergeant, Bill Hickman, suggested I see you. He said you were the best, and I needed the best to represent me."

Fellows rocked back in his overstuffed chair with a smile reminding me of a cat who just swallowed the canary. He placed his fingertips together making a teepee before speaking, "William said you were straight forward."

I think the surprised look on my face amused him as he stated, "William and I go back a long time. He didn't tell you, did he?"

He almost chuckled as he said, "We were political science majors at college. I went into law, and he went into police work. I tried to get him to apply to law school with me. He should have gone into law. He'd been an excellent lawyer. Has a sharp mind. We've remained close friends."

Margret interrupted the conversation bringing a coffee service and setting it on a long table at the side of the room. She poured two cups of coffee handing one to each of us. Without speaking a word, she left. The china cups and saucers were expensive. The cups walls were so thin I could see the level of the coffee through their sides. Again, I wondered if I could afford his services.

He took a small sip of coffee. He drank it black, like me, before continuing, "William contacted me late last night giving me his thoughts on the matter. He's very intuitive. I think he's correct. You're going to need me. I always advise my clients of one fact. The system is a court of law, not a court of justice"

I was suffering from information overload. Sergeant Hickman never mentioned his relationship with Fellows, ever! I blurted, "Mr. Fellows, I don't know if I can afford you!"

Once again, the slight smile before he answered, "I wouldn't be greatly concerned, John, if I may call you by your first name? I decided to represent you pro bono. Don't be mistaken, it's not strictly a humanitarian gesture. I believe this will be a high profile case. It's good for business... not that I need more clients, but my junior partners would gladly accept the referrals"

"This is an election year," Fellows said becoming very businesslike and serious. "The mayor and district attorney are up for re-election. If the mayor goes, historically, the police chief goes. The upper echelon will view this as a political matter with no regard of whether you're innocent or were thrust into a situation out of your control. From this point forward, do not speak with anybody about this matter without me present. Refer all inquiries to my office."

"What about my wife?" I asked.

"Of course you can talk to her. A wife can't be forced to testify against her husband. She has to keep it to herself though. But I caution you. Don't discuss it with any relatives or friends. Agreed?"

"I have to turn in a written report – departmental policy," I informed him.

"Make it as short and concise as possible... nothing but the facts... nothing that can draw speculation. Understood?" he asked.

The rest of the meeting involved me retelling the facts. Fellows would interrupt me asking a question while making a note on a yellow legal pad before allowing me to continue. He was thorough. I was mentally exhausted when it ended, but I had a glimmer of hope.

***

Sarah had been waiting at a nearby city park in her old silver grey Volvo station wagon. Her father had died when she was a young girl, and her mother had never remarried. Sarah said that her mother sometimes worked two jobs barely managing to make ends meet when she was young.

Her mother had scraped up enough money to buy the car for a graduation gift when Sarah finished her associate degree. It was the only good car we owned. My car should have been scrapped years ago, but it came in handy in a pinch.

Sarah picked me up on the sidewalk outside the attorney's office. We both had cell phones. I had called her as I was leaving his office. She pulled the car next to a parked car, blocking the traffic. As I jumped into the passenger's side, the driver behind her impatiently leaned on his horn. Sarah waved to the frustrated driver as she accelerated into the flow of traffic. "How'd it go?" she asked.

"There's some good news. Mr. Fellows volunteered to represent me pro bono, but he does have some concerns on how it will be presented on the news. He mentioned the mayor's up for re-election and would view it from a political standpoint."

Sarah was quiet as she thought about what I had said. She has a keen mind. Breaking the silence, she said, "In other words, the political masters are waiting to see how the news people spin the story. The officers on the street will close ranks and stand behind you because they know it could happen to them. But the big boys won't be willing to take the hit if a feeding frenzy starts. Am I correct?"

"That's it in a nutshell," I agreed.

"John," she paused weighing her words carefully. "This could get nasty. There could be wrongful death lawsuits filed by the families of either or both of the men who died. There are attorneys that'll jump at a chance to file. Of course you'll be named, but they'll be after the city's deep pockets. They'll settle for a fraction of what the suit states, and they know the city will pay because it's cheaper than the lawyer's bills. The fees would be staggering."

"If the city settles, does it take me out of the picture?" I asked.

"I don't know," she answered. "Remember, you told me you hadn't done the paperwork to work off duty. The city could try to use that as an excuse to say they're not responsible for your actions. We'll have to wait and see what happens."

There was no way I could express the gratitude I felt when she used the term we. I smiled and patted her on the knee as tears formed in my eyes. What's going on with me? I was crying again.

Sarah gave me a loving smile as her eyes flicked between me and the road. "It's OK to cry," she said compassionately. "John, you've got to realize you're a human being with emotions. If you try to keep them bottled inside, you'll eventually destroy yourself. I cried every day we were separated. It was as if half of my soul was missing, but now I feel whole again. Now I have some understanding of losing a mate through death."

I wiped the tears on my shirt sleeve and leaned over lightly kissing Sarah on the cheek. How had I been so foolish as to leave her? If I had not left her, then none of this would have ever happened. I wouldn't have needed the money and wouldn't have taken the job. But, if this tragedy hadn't taken place, we may have never reconciled. I slumped into the seat closing my eyes. I was too exhausted to think. Sleep overtook me.

***

It was 1:00 o'clock when Sarah shook me awake. We were parked in our driveway close to the side entrance. I was somewhat disoriented coming out of a deep sleep plus a terrible headache was disrupting my thinking ability. Through the fog I heard Sarah saying, "John, get up! That damn reporter is parked in front of our house! Be quick! Get into the house!"

As I opened the car door, I glanced seeing the reporter running across our lawn with a camera man in pursuit. Waving his arms trying to get my attention, he shouted, "Drake! John Drake! I need to talk to you!"

I bolted to the door, fishing the key out of my pants' pocket. In my peripheral I could see Sarah taking a blocking position between me and the reporter. The camera man had stopped to film the action. The reporter tried to sidestep Sarah, but she deftly mirrored his motion stopping him. As I entered the house, I heard snatches of a heated conversation. The reporter loudly directing questions towards me, "Why won't you talk to me? I just want to get your side of the story."

There was steel in Sarah's voice, "Officer Drake will be making no comments! If you want a statement, contact his attorney, Henry Fellows. Please leave our property!"

The reporter was being argumentative, "I just want some questions answered. The young man's family said he was a good person. The only reason he carried a gun was for defense. It's a rough a neighborhood. There have been a lot of shootings in that area. Two people are dead. Who shot the other officer?"

"You don't listen very well for a reporter," Sarah countered. "I've asked you to get off of our property. If you don't leave, I'm calling the police. I'll get a restraining order to keep you away. Your bosses won't like that."

The reporter sulked as he walked back to his car. Sarah came into the house pressing the door shut with her back. Leaning against the door with her arms across her bosom, she said, "It's starting. I'll bet the family already has an attorney. They're laying the groundwork."

Sarcastically she continued, "Poor kid. He had a rough upbringing. Never really did anything bad. It's society's fault because he wasn't provided the proper resources to be successful. If they hammer on that theme enough, there won't be a juror that won't be biased. They might claim to be unbiased, but the thought will be in the back of their minds."

"There's nothing I can do about that," I responded.

"You can't challenge the family directly, but there's other ways to discredit the bullshit they're feeding the press. There are a few reporters who support the police. Reporters who work the police beat are usually sympathetic with the police. They see what's going on. Let me feed the information to them. We'll keep you out of the picture as much as possible."

I didn't have a good feeling about what Sarah proposed, but I hadn't done very well on my own. Sarah had a feel for things like this. Things couldn't get much worse. I was wrong!

***

Sarah insisted on fixing me something to eat. As she was noisily gathering cooking utensils, I slumped into a chair at the table. I'd had little sleep. I recognized the symptoms of fatigue. I couldn't think clearly. My mouth started watering as the smell of bacon frying whiffed through the kitchen. Soon she placed a plate with three eggs, several strips of bacon and two pieces of toast in front of me with a glass of milk. After the first taste of egg, I was ravenous. Sarah fixed herself a cup of tea joining me at the table.

"You need to rest," she said. It was more of an order than a statement. "Eat, get a shower and go to bed. I'll wake you for supper."

I let the shower water run until it was hot enough to turn my skin a tinge pink. I used both hands to prop myself against the shower wall letting the water stream through my hair. I didn't think. The water running over my body had a soothing effect cleansing more than my body. I don't know how long I stood under the water, but it started turning cool. I had depleted the water supply in the hot water heater which was unusual for me. I take quick showers.

I took a towel off the rack smelling Sarah's scent when I put it to my face. I was home. How had I been foolish enough to have left? I finished drying wrapping the oversized towel around my waist. When I entered the bedroom, all my clothes were missing. Sarah came into the bedroom smiling at me. She said, "I'm washing your clothes. I want to lie beside you."

She moved to me draping her arms around me. Lightly kissing me, she said, "There's time for that later. I know how tired; you must be. I want to be with you. To touch you… John… I'm glad you're home."

Sarah could always read my thoughts. I wanted to make love to her, but I was physically depleted. It was unbelievable. I slid between the sheets curling into a ball. Sarah left her clothes on and lay on top of the sheets with an arm over my side. That's the last thing I remember before drifting into a dead man's sleep.

I felt something shaking my shoulder. I had trouble awakening. The first thought entering my mind was questioning where I was. Then I remembered. I was at home. I blinked my eyes several times before Sarah came into focus. She was sitting next to me with her hand on my shoulder. I slid my hand under her tee shirt working my way upwards. She shook her head but didn't stop me.

As I cupped her breast, she said, "John, there's nothing more than I'd rather do, but Sergeant Hickman's here. His timing is impeccably bad. Still, I think you better speak with him."

She stroked the side of my face before standing and leaving. My clothes were neatly folded at the foot of the bed. My whole body protested as I sat up. I felt feverish. If my past history held true, I'd get sick. After a severe stress, I would become ill. Perhaps it was a way for my body to punish me for putting myself in those situations. I was unsteady on my feet as I slowly dressed.

Looking at the alarm clock, I was surprise. It was 07:00 P.M. Damn, I had slept six hours.

CHAPTER 3

I was still wobbly as I entered the kitchen. To my surprise, Sergeant Hickman was sitting at the table dressed in street clothes drinking a mug of coffee. It dawned on me that I had never seen Hickman in civilian clothes. He looked different. He wasn't nearly as imposing without his uniform. Then it hit me. Strip the uniform off of him, and he is a man like a million others. I'd made a mistake common among people. I had thought my profession was what gave me worth. I realized I'm worth something because I'm a person.

Hickman started to rise, but I motioned for him to stay seated. I scanned the table seeing a manila file folder placed beside the coffee mug. It was new without any writing on it. Sarah handed me a mug of coffee before sitting at the table facing the sergeant. I couldn't read anything in Hickman's face.

As he started speaking, I noted his tone. He spoke as a mentor. It wasn't a condescending tone, but an experienced man sharing his knowledge with a neophyte, "John, I'm pleased you're back with your wife."

I knew it was common knowledge we were separated, but it puzzled me where he was going with the conversation. I resented him bringing up the subject, especially in front of my wife as he continued, "I've been married thirty-three years. Police work is not conducive to marriage. You must have your priorities in order. My philosophy is very simple. God comes first, then my wife, family and job, in that order."

"I believe it takes a special person to be a police officer. We consider ourselves warriors. In fact, we are warriors. But, we have to learn how to balance our lives. Many officers never have a stable relationship. The quality of the people we interact with on a daily basis tends to make us cynical. Some officers have long term relationships without going through the legalities. I don't judge them. The point I'm making is they have a support base. They have somebody who loves them enough to listen to them vent their frustrations. I find myself needing this support. If you think I'm out of line, I apologize, but I felt it needed to be said."

I was perplexed. Sarah was nodding in agreement, intently studying me. I felt blood rushing to my face as I began to blush. It wasn't from anger. It was from embarrassment. He was stating a fact I should have known. He wasn't chastising me. He was sharing an imitate detail of his life in order to help me. Why share this information with me? Was I being a cynic? I decided to take it at face value. He was trying to help. I felt my face returning to its normal color.

Appearing not to notice my reaction, he continued, "You're a good officer. You'll be a better officer once this is over. Metal gets strengthened every time it is thrust into the fire. You *will* be stronger after this is over. I want to show you something.

"I want you to give this information to Mr. Fellows. He can use it however he deems appropriate. It can't be traced back to you or me because Fellows doesn't have to reveal where he got the information. I believe it falls under client attorney privilege. Any conversation or information passed between you and your attorney is confidential. Nobody is going to push that point.

"The news people are all over this. At the present, the brass is holding the line saying it's under investigation, etcetera. That's a positive point, but they're not saying it's a righteous shooting. The preliminary report from homicide has to be sitting on their desks. Looking at the shooting from their viewpoint, it isn't a clear cut case. There are too many things that can't be explained. Considering the facts as they are today, it appears you shot Frank."

"I didn't shoot Frank!" I said loudly.

"I didn't say you did," he countered. "The key word you missed was appears. Personally, I don't believe you shot Frank. Let's wait for the forensic and coroner reports. We'll talk more about it after we see the reports."

I couldn't believe Hickman didn't seem overly concerned about whether I had or had not shot a fellow police officer. Was I reading him wrong? Before I had a chance to ask for an explanation, he continued, "The news people love a complicated shooting like this. If given the chance, they'll try to convict you in the media. There's one reporter you want to avoid, Jacob Bellows. I don't know anything about his past history, but he hammers the police every time he's given a chance."

Sarah interrupted, "He's already tried to interview John. He shoved a card at me when I asked him to leave. He said to give him a call when John wants his side of the story told."

"Sounds like his tactics," commented Hickman as he opened the file. "The perp with the gun was Dejuan Treece, aka Ghetto Dog. Nineteen years old. Member of the Perros. They started out as a two bit gang, but they've been expanding their turf. They're heavily into the drug trade.

"He was a bad dude according to my buddies in narcotics. He was nothing but trouble. Dropped out of school in the eighth grade when he turned sixteen. His court records were sealed when he turned eighteen. Since then, he had two minor convictions for trafficking in marijuana and an assault charge. The victim dropped the assault charge. Narcotics figure the victim was intimidated.

"Rumor on the street is that he was with another gang member named Ali Johnson, aka Little Dog. We think Johnson was his gopher. He carried the dope for Treece and would take the fall if they were busted. But, we really don't know their relationship besides being in the same gang.

"Treece was a suspect in two drive-by shootings. Homicide can't build a case because the neighborhood peeps are afraid to testify. Apparently, he's moved up the food chain. Narcotics think they were carrying a large enough quantity of dope that both of them would have been charged with trafficking.

"It'd be interesting to know what drugs the coroner found in his blood. With possession of a firearm while selling, he'd be facing a Class C felony. There's no way he'd want to spend ten years in the pen. He knew he'd be going away for a long time if you busted him. He was going to use the gun. John, you didn't have a choice. He would have killed both of you."

25

The facts that Hickman had given would lead the average person to the conclusion that I had justification for the shooting. I felt relieved until Sarah spoke, "Sergeant Hickman, it's obvious to us that he was a dangerous man. Nobody else will know how dangerous he was, except for the police who had to deal with him.

"I don't believe the press will bother to dig too deeply. His two minor convictions for marijuana will be blown off because he was underprivileged. I watched the six o'clock news. They had a special interview with his parents who said Dejuan was studying for his GED, and they showed a picture of him in a suit. They said he was planning to go to college after he got his GED. His parents said he'd never hurt anybody. He carried a gun because of the neighborhood."

"I never said it was going to be easy," answered Hickman.

***

Hickman wouldn't stay for dinner. I decided to take Sarah for pizza. Sarah made arrangements with her mother to keep Amy for the night. In my mind, we were celebrating being together again. We decided to go to a small family owned Italian restaurant. It was in an old building, small compared to restaurants like today's standards and very private. We were greeted by an older white haired man as we entered. He seemed genuinely pleased to see us. We used to eat there frequently. I asked him to seat us where we could have some privacy. He led us through the narrow restaurant to a booth by itself in the very back.

I slid across the worn leather seat. I don't know why, but it was comforting. It wasn't like sitting on the modern plastic or polished wooden seats in the new cookie cutter establishments. Maybe it was the ambiance of the well used décor giving the impression of enduring stability. Then I realized the significance was being with Sarah. She was the rock that gave me stability.

We ordered a carafe of red house wine with a medium sausage pizza. Sarah took a sip of wine savoring the flavor as she rolled it on her tongue. Slowly swirling the wine in her glass, she said, "We need to go by the apartment to get your clothes and personal effects. The rest we can worry about later."

I reluctantly agreed to go after the meal. During dinner, we chatted about Amy. My daughter was becoming more of an individual with each passing day. I could have missed the joy of being part of her life. The more I listened, the more I was determined to be part of the family. It's odd how a tragedy can bring a family together. It made me realize what is truly important in life. As we approached the apartment, I saw a group of well dressed individuals mulling in the parking area. There was no doubt in my mind. The sharks smelled blood in the water, and they were gathering for the kill. Sarah drove past the apartment saying, "Maybe this wasn't such a good idea. The press is camped at the apartment."

A dread welled up inside me. It was close to a fear. It's OK to be scared, but police can't let fear rule their actions; otherwise, they would be paralyzed and couldn't perform their duty. We're not fearless, but we use fear to make us cautious in the manner of how we approach a situation. Some cops call it a gut feeling. I call it falling back on your training.

Pushing the fear and dread into an isolated part of my brain, I said, "Turn around and go back to the apartment. I'm going to have to face them sooner or later."

I could see by Sarah's expression she didn't want to go back. She drove into a filling station placing the car in park. Turning to face me, she said, "I can go back by myself. I'll gather a few things and come back for you."

"That's just delaying the inevitable," I answered. "We'll keep our heads down and go straight to the apartment. We don't have to answer any questions."

***

Sarah parked close to the apartment's hallway entrance. The reporters identified me immediately from the standard picture the department issues when situations like this arise. It was as if a herd of zombies surrounded us. The lights on the cameras were blazing in our faces. I was temporarily blinded by camera flashes. This told me video and print reporters were present.

A microphone was roughly shoved into my face. Someone shouted, "Do you want to tell us your side of the story! Did you shoot your partner?'

Turning away, I mumbled, "No comment."

I saw Sarah was trapped by the reporters. They had boxed her against the car. I pushed through the crowd reaching Sarah with some difficulty. Taking her hand, I started leading her through the reporters. A hand firmly grabbed my shoulder. Training took over. Cops can't allow people to place hands on them. People will hurt cops. I grabbed the thumb twisting it clockwise until the palm faced upwards. Jacob Bellows was bent facing the pavement screaming. I had him in a wrist and elbow lock with his arm levered upwards.

Sarah screamed, "Let him go John!"

Oh shit! What have I done? It was muscle memory. I didn't think. I reacted from training. We constantly practice defensive maneuvers to subdue a suspect quickly. We're taught the longer the struggle the more likely either the cop or the suspect will be injured. I released Bellows' hand backing away from him. Bellows rubbed his elbow as he righted himself. I could see hate in his eyes as he growled, "You had no right to do that! You over reacted! Is that what happened?"

Before I could respond, Sarah pushed between us glaring at Bellows. "You had no right to lay hands on him!" she shouted angrily.

"The public has a right to know what happened!" Bellows responded raising his voice to match Sarah's.

"Then wait for the investigation to be completed. Maybe you can get your facts straight!" she retaliated.

I held firmly to Sarah's hand bulling through the crowd half dragging her behind me. The zombies had their bite of flesh for today. I wasn't giving them anymore to eat. I knew Bellows would beat the drum of police brutality and over reacting. I hadn't helped my cause. The clip of me twisting his arm would be aired over and over. I didn't realize it would make national news. The networks liked nothing better than a cop beating up a reporter who was just trying to do his job. It's good for ratings.

The reporters followed us to the apartment shouting questions. We kept our eyes forward as if they were not present. Once inside, I said, "I screwed up big time."

"The jerk got what he deserved," Sarah answered.

She was still angry and not thinking clearly. She was correct, but the news wouldn't address that point. He didn't have the right to lay hands on me. Shit! The mayor and chief weren't going to like this. Way to go John!

***

The crowd of reporters had diminished by the time we gathered four large black garbage bags of clothes along with a few toilet articles. There were a few camera flashes as we dumped the bags on the backseat, but nobody approached us. The television reporters must have returned to their respective stations to edit their clips for the late evening news. We drove most of the way home in silence with each of us lost in our own thoughts. Sarah was the first to speak, "Bellows is an asshole. I know we're not going to like it, but we should watch him on the late news. It might not be as bad as we think. He was just as wrong as you were."

Staring into the darkness, I answered, "It doesn't matter if he was wrong. It's how he presents it. He's not going to make himself look like an ass. He'll crucify me. I'll become unclean as far as the upper echelon is concerned."

There were no cars parked close to our house as Sarah pulled into the driveway. We carried the bags into our bedroom placing them on the floor. There would time to unpack them tomorrow. As I dug my razor out of a bag, Sarah turned on the small television on her dresser. The ten o'clock news was beginning. A photograph of me in my uniform flashed onto the screen behind Jacob Bellows. She turned up the volume.

Jacob Bellows was smugly looking directly into the camera. He said, "Tonight, I tried to interview Officer John Drake about the multiple shootings which took place at the Double H Lounge. This reporter had asked him a simple question – had he accidentally shot a fellow officer? I'll let the video clip speak for itself."

The clip started with me twisting Bellows' wrist as his face contorted in pain. At the end of the clip, the camera had panned to my face. I had a savage expression which was frozen on the screen. Using this as a backdrop, Bellows stated, "I admit I lightly touched him trying to get his attention, but I consider this an abuse of force. He could have simply walked away from me. This makes one question how he reacted at the Double H Lounge. Did he over-react? This is a question the police chief needs to answer. When will we get some answers? This is Jacob Bellows reporting for Channel 12 news."

29

The next segment of the news showed our local civil rights activist, Ali 3X, with his twelve local supporters picketing in front of police headquarters. It was always the same twelve people. The camera was zoomed in on Ali 3X with his supporters bunched around him which made it look like a large protest. For a man with no visible means of monetary support, he dressed well. His suit didn't come off a sales rack. Of course, the businesses which made donations to his organization were never picketed for civil right abuses. The press turned a blind eye to that.

Then the news had a statement from the chief of police. He read a prepared statement refusing to answer questions because the case was under investigation. However, the mayor used it as an opportunity, "As the mayor, I deeply regret any time there's a shooting in our city. I have the utmost confidence in our chief to thoroughly conduct an investigation without prejudice. Justice will be done."

I turned the television off. I wanted to throw up. Sarah was sitting at the foot of the bed. She had gone completely pale. In a sobbing voice, she said, "He's as much as accused you of over-reacting at the shootings."

"I'm sure the station's attorneys reviewed his little speech before he gave it," I said. "He's peddling doubt. Nothing you can legally do. Can't sue him for libel for questioning what happened even if he's subtly leading the viewer to a conclusion."

"I'm glad you're not like him," she said moving to embrace me. Our bodies melted into one. We made an urgent and passionate love that night, not only renewing the union between a man and a woman but also between a husband and wife. No matter the outcome. No matter the consequences. We had each other.

CHAPTER 4

It was Saturday morning. Both of us slept late. Sarah had gone to full time at the law offices to make ends meet. Thankfully, she was off on weekends. The phone jarred us awake. It was on Sarah's side so she answered it. After a curt conversation, she shook her head as she handed the phone to me. I figured whoever was on the other side didn't have good news. Sitting up with the sheets covering me, I said, "Hello."

The voice on the phone said, "This is Sergeant Watkins from vehicle pool. Am I speaking to Officer John Drake?"

"Yes it is," I answered.

"I need to know the location of your take home unit so I can send some people to pick it up," Watkins stated bluntly. "You don't have to meet them. You can turn in your key the next time you're at headquarters."

The vehicle pool has duplicate keys for all police vehicles. Watkins' tone of voice told me two things without him saying it. He didn't like repossessing my take home, and he didn't want to talk about it. I gave him the address to the apartment informing him I had no personal gear in the car. He said he would send people to get it immediately and hung up. I understood. From his perspective, he was in a field of corn – too many ears. People fill-in the blanks on a one sided conversation. Too often, the blanks are filled-in wrong.

Sarah was in the bathroom brushing her teeth. She was furiously working the tooth brush. I guess it was her way of releasing some frustration. I hugged her from behind laying my cheek on top of her head before explaining, "The vehicle pool is picking up the take home unit. It's no big deal. Standard procedure."

I didn't know if it was standard procedure or not because I've never been suspended, but I didn't want Sarah to worry. I was concerned. Why had they repossessed it so quickly? Wouldn't they wait until the investigation was completed? Or, had the powers that be already decided my fate? I reminded myself not to jump to conclusions. This was an unwritten play. It would unfold one act at a time. I had to wait to know the ending.

"John, it doesn't feel right," she said through a mouth full of foamy toothpaste. "I think they're trying to distance themselves from you. They're moving you out the door in incremental steps. They took your badge, ID and car."

"I don't know what's going to happen," I answered. "I feel powerless."

Sarah rinsed the toothpaste out of her mouth then began brushing her hair while watching me in the mirror, "I suspect the chief and mayor saw Bellows last night. They're not willing to take the heat. I'll bet their phone lines were burning up last night. You're expendable. The elections are in four months. The mayor doesn't want this interfering with his re-election. If the mayor goes, then so does the police chief. It's all political."

"There's nothing I can do about it. I'm still constrained from talking to reporters by policy. Only the department's information officer can talk to the press," I said watching her reaction in the mirror.

"You can't," she said turning to face me. "But I sure as hell can! I don't work for the police department!"

Sarah was fired up. I knew that no amount of reasoning would change her mind. In all likelihood we'd end in an argument. I didn't want a fight. We had just gotten back together. I kissed her on the forehead before leaving to fix us some coffee.

***

We had a light breakfast while planning our day. Sarah's mood lightened during breakfast. She was going to drop me off at the apartment before picking up Amy at her parents' house. I was going to load up the few food supplies I had plus the rest of my clothes in my car. Hopefully, the P.O.S. would start. If there were reporters hanging around, I'd cross that bridge when I came to it. I was looking forward to playing with Amy later.

When we arrived at the apartment, I saw the spot where my take home unit had been parked was empty. The sergeant was true to his word. He hadn't wasted any time getting the car. I waved to Sarah as she drove away. I hesitated before going in the apartment. It held too many unwanted memories. When I turned the doorknob before putting the key in the lock, I realized it was unlocked. I knew I had locked it when we left last night.

The hair stood up on the back of my neck. Somebody could be in the apartment. I didn't have a gun or any weapon to defend myself if they were still there. I pushed the door open. I didn't know what I'd do if somebody was in there armed. A well groomed man, whom I judged to be in his late twenties, was sitting in my overstuffed chair. He wore an expensive looking pullover shirt, tailored slacks and highly polished loafers. He wasn't the typical burglar.

"I was banking on you coming back this morning," he said not bothering to rise.

"Who the hell are you?" I stammered taken back by his nonchalant attitude of being there.

"First, let me tell you who I'm not. I'm not some reporter trying to make a name for myself by hanging you out to dry," he answered with a serious expression on his face. "But I am a reporter. My name is Mark Mumford."

I interrupted him stepping through the doorway towards him, "Get out! I can have you arrested for breaking and entering."

Mumford held up both hands as if surrendering, "Please, give me just one minute to explain. My father and brother are police officers in another state. I come from a long line of police officers. You're going to take a fall unless you get some help, and I'm willing to help."

"I've already gotten all the help I need from the news people," I snarled.

"I understand you feelings," he said calmly. "Bellows did a number on you. Remember the old admonishment about throwing stones if you live in a glass house. Bellows is carrying baggage. My father saw the clip on national news. He remembered Bellows having run-ins with the law – two DUI's and an assault charge. It's nothing personal against you. He hates all police. He blames them because he was fired from his last job. He got too much bad PR from the arrests."

I stood frozen with my mouth open. Was this guy for real or trying to gain my confidence in order to get a story? Mumford smiled as he laid a business card on an end table, "I was here last night. I witnessed what Bellows did. The way he grabbed you, he was lucky he didn't get punched. Watch the news on Channel 46 tonight at six o'clock. It should convince you I'm on your side. I know you're not supposed talk to me, but if you have any sources…"

He left the words hang as he skirted around me and left the apartment. I shut the door and locked it. I went to the couch picking up his card. I sat on the couch staring at his card. I had to think.

***

Sarah was home with Amy when I arrived. At eighteen months, Amy was beginning to become very mobile. She didn't have my dark eyes and hair, but neither did she have Sarah's light features. Amy's hair was a fawn color with matching eyes. When I entered the house, she took a misstep falling on her rear which was amply padded with a diaper. I swept her off the floor holding her above my head listening to her laughter. She was the most beautiful little girl I had ever seen.

Sarah watched us play for a few seconds before saying, "John, you're going to have to stop spoiling her."

I knew Sarah didn't mean it because she was smiling. After putting Amy back on the floor, I told Sarah about Mumford. Wrinkling her brow, she said, "I think he's the new reporter on Channel 46. He's supposed to be an investigative reporter – whatever that means. I don't know if we can trust him."

"Let's watch him on the news tonight. Then we can make some kind of decision on what to do," I answered.

"John, you're not going to be able to discuss the shooting with him. You've always told me, as an officer, you weren't allowed to talk to the press. You had to notify the information officer. Then, he spoke with the press. If they found out you were talking with Mumford, in itself it would be grounds for disciplinary action. Am I wrong?"

"Doesn't appear that Mumford can be much help," I commented.

34

"Not necessarily true," Sarah said wagging a finger in front of me. "I don't work for the police. They can't tell me who I can or cannot speak to. Let's see how he approaches the shootings on the news before making any kind of decision."

The day went by in a flash. My father came to our house instead of calling. He came without my mother. I steeled myself for a lecture ending with "I told you so". But he didn't comment about the police other than to ask if I was OK. He didn't inquire about the shootings. He didn't ask about what was going to happen. He acted as if Sarah and I had never been separated. I guess he figured I had enough on my plate without him adding to it. He mostly played with his granddaughter. He had tears in his eyes when he hugged me before he left. That was strange. My father never displayed his emotions.

As I watched him back his car out of the driveway, I suddenly felt guilty about the way I had felt about him. I thought of Dad as a hard man, but he was reared in hard times. He was a product of those times; however, he just demonstrated something I had never realized. Although he didn't appreciate my career choice, he still loved and supported me. I was his son regardless of my choices and regardless of the consequences of those choices.

I felt like the prodigal son. My father had never left me. I had left him. Now I had returned.

***

We had the small television on the kitchen counter tuned to Channel 46 as we ate supper. Amy was smearing food on the tray of her highchair. Sarah and I had given up. It was easier to bathe her afterwards. I wasn't sure whether there was more food in her or on the tray. The news at six promised an investigative report on the shootings. After all the intros, Mumford appeared on the screen. Behind him was a large picture of Sarah and me. We were trapped against our car by a mass of reporters.

Mumford had a stern expression saying, "I am an investigative reporter. My responsibility is to report the facts. I do not report the facts as I would like them to be. I report the facts as they are presented. When I believe the facts have been manipulated to sensationalize, it is a matter of ethics that I present the other side of the story."

Mumford paused for either effect or to give the viewers time to digest what he had said before continuing, "Officer John Drake was involved in the shooting at the Double H Lounge where two men died. One man was armed. The second man was a police officer. The matter is under investigation by the police department. As a seasoned reporter, I know that an officer cannot speak with me while the investigation is active. However, I can still ask questions. Sometimes an officer will make a comment. No foul committed by asking.

"However, there are unwritten rules that have to be observed. I can ask a question, but I cannot force a person to respond. The person is not to lay hands upon me for asking the question even if the person believes the question inflammatory or unjust. Isn't the reverse true for me? An ethical dilemma has been laid at my feet. An issue has been raised by another news organization insinuating Officer Drake overreacted and used excessive force."

Again Mumford paused creating a dramatic effect before saying, "Our film crew was at the scene when the officer supposedly overreacted. I decided not to cast my opinion but to let the viewers decide for themselves. The video I'm about to show may give the viewer a different perspective. You, the viewer, be the judge. What would you have done in this situation?"

The television screen filled with reporters jostling Sarah and me. It showed Bellows bulling his way to the front forcefully grabbing my shoulder spinning me to face him. Bellows looked angry. My reaction and movement was so fast that it appeared as a blur as I put Bellows in an arm lock. A look of horror appeared on my face when I recognized what I had done. I immediately released him. Bellows' face went from pain to smug satisfaction. Then, Sarah interceded.

Mumford reappeared on the screen. He retained the stern expression saying, "If you want to view this video clip again, it is available on our website. Also, we are taking a poll on our website. You can vote whether the officer overreacted, or if his actions were justified. This is Mark Mumford, investigative reporter, Channel 46 news."

We both sat staring at the television. Sarah used the remote to turn off the television. "What do you think?" I asked.

"Highly unusual," she answered. "Mumford came as close to supporting you as he could without saying it. He's taking a risk. He could be viewed as a Judas by the other reporters. I'm surprised the station's management let him do it."

I considered what Sarah said. It was a calculated move. They were the top two stations in the area. It was a ratings war. If Mumford could show the other station was unreliable in their reporting, then his station would gain viewers. I was positive the war would heat up. I hoped I wouldn't be caught in the middle.

***

I told Sarah I needed to be by myself for awhile. I drove my old rattletrap car aimlessly letting my mind wander. A faint trail of blue followed the car. It burned half a quart of oil with each tank of gas. It wasn't a conscious decision, but I ended up driving by the Double H Lounge. It looked crowded. Apparently the shooting hadn't affected business. It very well might have helped their business.

A certain category of people are drawn to violence and tragedies. It's like the people who chase fire trucks. Fires are tragedies. Homes are lost, but at every fire there are spectators. Some are pyromaniacs at heart. Some are thrill seekers. It doesn't matter. They're there cluttering up the scene. It's the same mentality at shootings.

I made a U turn and headed back towards the bar. Pulling my car to the curb a half a block from the bar, I turned off the engine watching the activity through the windshield. I sat watching for thirty minutes or so. A few people would stop and point at the sidewalk where Frank had bled out. His blood must have stained the concrete. It'd fade and disappear with time. Most things did – even memories.

It was a stupid thing to do. I knew it was stupid when I got out of my car. I couldn't stop myself. I went into the bar to ask the bar girls if they had seen anything. The bartender saw me as soon as I entered. He was a large man with a shaved head and a goatee. His arms and neck were covered with tattoos. He motioned me to the bar. He sat a drink in front of me which I pushed away. Shrugging his shoulders, he picked up the glass taking a sip from it. In a low voice, he said, "I never paid you."

Before I could speak, he turned walking to the cash register. He opened the drawer palming a few bills. He came back laying the money in front of me. I pushed the bills back to him saying," I don't want the money."

Again, he shrugged his shoulders picking up the money. He folded the bills tucking them in his shirt pocket before asking, "What do you want?"

"Did any of the girls see anything?" I asked.

"Haven't heard them say anything," he answered again shrugging his shoulders.

"Mind if I talk to Brandy?" I asked.

"She doesn't work here anymore," he said with a faint smile flickering on his lips. "She quit today. Didn't leave any forwarding information so I can't tell you how to get in touch with her."

I knew this was leading to a dead end. The bartender wasn't going to tell me anything. He left to make a phone call at the opposite end of the bar. A bar girl, whom I didn't recognize, slid onto the stool next to me. Sizing me up, she asked, "You're the cop who killed those two last night?"

"I didn't kill two," I answered harshly.

Without another word, she slid off the stool sauntering off to another man at the bar. I ordered a soft drink and sat watching the activity. The girls were working. A careless hand brushing a man's crotch. A breast pressed against the back of a man's shoulder. It was a not so subtle invitation. It was an invitation that came with a price. I laid two dollars on the bar beside the untouched soft drink. It really was stupid being here.

***

The fresh air felt good as I walked outside. I could smell the stale cigarette smoke hanging on my clothes. I needed a long shower to rid myself of the smell. There was a light breeze causing my oversized tee shirt to flap. The air had the distinct smell of rain approaching. I aimlessly wandered down the sidewalk to where Frank had been shot. A dark stain was all the physical evidence that remained. The blood stain was much larger than I expected.

I was astonished about how much blood Frank has lost. It was amazing how quickly life could flow out of a person. The impending rain would probably wash away the stain. I wished the whole incident could be erased as easily as I turned to walk back to my car. I felt it before I heard the report of the gun. Something snagged the side of my tee shirt briefly.

Then I heard the loud retort of a firearm. I was bewildered for a second before my brain registered I had been shot at, but I wasn't hit.

I jumped behind a telephone pole peaking around it. A muzzle blast lighted up the alley next to the far side of the bar. A loud thump reverberated through the massive wooden pole showering splinters. Shit! Somebody's trying to kill me! From training, I knew the telephone pole was more concealment than cover. Too much of me was exposed. It was fight or flight time. It is incredible how quickly the mind reacts to danger.

I didn't have a weapon to defend myself so the only option left was to flee. If I remained behind the pole, I would eventually be hit. I was soaked with sweat as my body prepared for fleeing. I sprang between two cars zigzagging into the street. A car window exploded behind me. I sprinted down the street randomly jerking in opposite directions. Car horns blared as the cars swerved to miss me. The whole scene was surreal. I felt like everything was moving in slow motion.

I had never run so fast in my whole life. I covered two city blocks in seconds before realizing there were no more shots. Ducking behind some large shrubs, I peaked around their edges to see if anybody was following. The street was empty of people. Cars moved rapidly up and down the street as if nothing had happened. I suppose the drivers thought it was another crazy drunk running in the street. As a police officer, I've seen intoxicated people in the street many times. We'd arrest them for alcohol intoxication because they were more harmful to themselves than anything else. A car would eventually hit them.

Something puzzled me. I didn't hear any sirens. My puzzlement cleared after a second of rational thought. There were gunshot sounds in this part of the city consistently. It happened often, and we couldn't respond unless a complaint was called in. The noise in the alley may have been mistaken for a firecracker. The sound of the car window breaking was probably masked by the noise. Finally I heard the sounds of a siren approaching.

Digging my cell phone out of my pocket, I hit the speed dial for the police radio room. When a dispatcher answered, I spoke quickly running my words together, "This is Officer Drake, badge 466, shots fired at the Double H Lounge!" I've been shot at!"

The dispatcher's voice remained monotone as she asked, "Have you been shot?"

"No," I answered starting to calm down enough to answer in a reasonable tone of voice.

"Has anybody else been injured?"

"I don't know."

"A complaint has been called in, and a unit is on the way. I'll notify the unit that a police officer is involved. How are you dressed?"

"I'm wearing a grey tee shirt and blue jeans with tennis shoes," I answered.

She asked my location and told me to stay where I was a until a unit arrived. Now I heard other sirens approaching. When the call went out on the radio that an officer was shot at, every nearby available unit would respond. An officer in trouble could depend on his brother and sister officers for help. We are a family. Family members protect each other.

CHAPTER 5

Two marked units came screaming towards the bar from the direction facing me. They killed their sirens as they stopped by the car with its window shattered. I could see the officers cautiously come out of their cars. They had their weapons drawn with their flashlights sweeping the area. A third unit approached behind me with emergency lights but no siren. The unit's bright spotlight lighted the yards as it drove slowly towards me. I stepped onto the sidewalk with my hands held up. The spotlight engulfed me. I was temporarily blinded while the officer decided if I was a threat.

The spotlight flickered off as the unit glided to the curb with the passenger window opening. I recognized the voice. It was J.B. Madison. Everybody called him JB. He shouted, "John, what in the hell are you doing here?"

I gaped at him like I was in a stupor. He shook his head either in disgust or loathing. Both of us knew I had created more trouble for myself. It was incredulously stupid on my part. No matter what I said, there would be speculation.

JB motioned me to get in the backseat. His car had a cage making me feel like a criminal. This was a clear signal he considered me a civilian, not a fellow officer, or he was just covering his ass. A fellow officer would have been invited to ride in the front seat. I reflected what I would have done if the roles were reversed. He drove to the front of the bar getting out to open the rear door. The rear door of a patrol car can't be opened from the inside to keep prisoners from escaping.

I climbed out of the car walking to a group of officers huddled around the smashed car window. JB closely followed. The rear window had a large hole with spider webs in the glass spreading from the hole. The driver's window was shattered with shards blown out on the street. Obviously a large caliber bullet had done the damage. The bullet had been distorted going through the first sheet of glass expending its kinetic energy on the second window.

There were three uniforms and one suit examining the damage. I knew the suit. He was Kenneth Wilson. He had gone through the academy with me. Wilson had recently transferred to the homicide unit. Wilson motioned me to him with a perplexed look on his face. He waited for me to come to him before saying, "I'd say you had a close call." He placed a finger through one of the holes in the side of my shirt.

I looked down at his finger in the hole. I'd damn near been killed! My knees began to buckle as I felt light headed and reality set in. Strong hands grasped me under my arms lowering me to the pavement. I heard somebody ask if I were hurt. I mumbled something. I don't remember what I said. Hands searched all over my body probing for a wound. After they were satisfied I was OK, a bottle of water was thrust into my hand. I gratefully took a sip.

As I regained my wits, Wilson squatted beside me with a notepad in his hand. Preparing to take notes, he asked, "Let's start with the four W's – who, when, where, and why. The when and where is answered. I'm curious about who and why. John, why are you here, and who would try to kill you?"

By now, the news people were arriving. Great! My picture would in the paper again. The uniforms were stringing the yellow police tape around the crime scene while trying to keep reporters and spectators at bay. I heard one of the reports shout, "That's John Drake! He's the same officer involved in the shooting here last night!"

The connection had been made. What would they print? All kinds of conjectures and suppositions could be spun. It could go for or against me according to the spin put on the story. Wilson helped me to my feet guiding me to the sidewalk while using the car as a shelter between us and the reporters.

After I told him everything that had happened, he flipped the notepad shut saying, "You should have stayed away from here. However, this puts a different twist on the whole incident. Somebody is trying to get payback. I'd suspect it's the perp's peeps. He was a gangbanger and was part of a gang who call themselves the "Perros". It's Spanish for dogs. Bastards probably view you blowing him away as a matter of disrespect. This is a way of gaining back the respect in the gangs' eyes."

"Just what I need!" I spat.

"Let me get the crime scene techs. I can see where a bullet hit the telephone pole. At least we'll have the slug. With a little luck, the weapon might have been used in another crime."

Lowering his voice to a whisper, Wilson continued, "Strictly off the record, we're shaking down every lead on the other shooting. That son of a bitch was going to shoot you. We know he was the shooter in two drive-bys. We just can't prove it. I'm hunting for his buddy. He's gone to ground. We can't find him. When I do catch up with him, I'll squeeze his nuts so hard he'll sing soprano. I'll get the truth out of the scumbag."

Wilson and I walked to the alley where I had seen the muzzle flash. He did a thorough sweep of the corner of the alley looking for evidence. There were no empty shell casings. This told me the gunman was using a revolver, not a semi-automatic pistol. There was no way the shooter could have retrieved the empty casings without being seen. A pistol ejects the spent casings several feet. Wilson had told me only my spent casings had been found at the other shooting. Was it the same shooter?

***

Wilson had a phalanx of uniforms escort me to my car keeping the reporters at bay. At my car, I retrieved a tee shirt out of the gym bag in my trunk. The detective wanted my tee shirt for evidence. Bright flashes of light kept blinding me from reporters taking pictures. I gave the shirt to a uniform to deliver to Wilson. Other uniforms blocked the street so that I could ease my car onto the street. Once I was moving, I didn't stop to look at the scene. Reporters were running beside the car trying to snap pictures. I accelerated leaving them behind.

I called Sarah on my cell for two reasons. First, if she heard about it on the news, she'd be worried I was hurt. Second, I wanted to tell her what really happened. I was positive the news would put a different spin on the story. She answered on the first ring asking, "John, are you OK?"

That answered my first concern. It was already on the news, and she knew about it. "I'm fine. Somebody took a couple of shots at me. I have no idea why. I don't want to talk about it on the cell. I'll tell you everything when I get home. I'm on my way now."

"OK," she said lingering for a few seconds before disconnecting.

I was driving on automatic pilot. My mind was elsewhere. Although Detective Wilson brought up the gang angle, it didn't make sense to me. A gang would have more likely done a drive-by shooting, non-discriminately spraying the area hoping to hit me. To me, it was an act of an individual. One question kept rattling around in my head. Who would want to kill me besides the gang members? Was this an opportunistic crime? A crazy believing he was delivering justice?

My cell phone rang several times breaking me out of my trance. I saw on the caller ID it was Sergeant Hickman. I was tempted not to answer, but I did because Hickman was an allied, "This is John, Sarge."

"I spoke with Detective Wilson," said Hickman running his words together like a rapid firing machine gun. "If it's OK with you, I'm coming to your house and talk. You can call your wife and tell her to expect me."

I told him I'd be home in a few minutes. He may have asked if it was OK for him to come, but he hadn't given me a choice. It was an order more or less by his last statement. Hickman had something on his mind. I didn't need another reminder of how stupid I had been. I called Sarah telling her to expect him. I was surprised by her response. She thought it was a good idea.

I pulled my car into our driveway placing it in park as I let the motor idle. I looked at my watch. It was 12:30 A.M. I turned the motor off slowly climbing out of the car. Another car's headlights rapidly approached. It was a marked unit. It had to be the Sarge. He was getting off middle shift which ended at mid night. The car pulled behind mine, and the Sergeant got out. He was still in uniform. He hadn't taken time to change.

Hickman walked towards me saying, "You've had a hell of a night!"

I shook my head waving him to follow. Sarah had the side door open without the porch light burning. She was silhouetted by the interior light. I was back at safe harbor. I gave her a light kiss on the lips as I entered the house. In turn, she gave me a firm hug which was very reaffirming.

***

Sarah had ham and cheese sandwiches on the table with glasses of iced tea. I wasn't cognizant of how hungry I was until I took the first bite. Hickman sipped the tea from his glass ignoring the sandwiches. As I was chewing, he said, "John, I want you to tell me everything that happened from the time you parked at the Double H Lounge until you left. Don't leave out anything whether you think it has a bearing or not. Understand?"

I wolfed the sandwich following it with a half a glass of tea. I didn't speak for a few seconds gathering my thoughts. Hickman had a notepad with a pen in hand poised to take notes. As I relayed the chain of events, he scribbled a few notes on the pad. When something sparked his interest, he stopped me and had me expound.

After I had finished, he studied his notepad before saying, "There's a few things that strike me as being out of the norm. We need to find the girl named Brandy. What does she know that's important enough for her to disappear?"

Trying to approach the subject as tactfully as possible, I said, "I think she had something going on with Frank. Maybe she didn't want that brought out."

"What makes you suspect that?" he asked.

"She was all over him during the night, and they went to the parking lot to his car for about half an hour. I saw the same pattern with several of the bar girls," I answered.

With disdain clearly in his voice, he asked, "And you didn't suspect there was prostitution taking place?"

It wasn't the time to hedge with the sergeant so I answered truthfully, "I figure they were taking the tricks out to the cars, but I didn't go outside to confirm what I suspected. I didn't want to know."

"You should have left then and there," he bluntly stated. "Nothing can be done about it now, but it puts a different light on the matter. If Frank was involved with her, she could have been blackmailing him for favors. Or, he could have been extorting sex out of her. I rather doubt the first scenario, but if the latter was the case, then her pimp wouldn't like it. It'd cost the pimp a lot of money. She couldn't service Johns with Frank hanging around. Still... I can't see a pimp shooting a police officer."

"It's no secret that Frank liked the women," Hickman continued. "The bartender was handing you a bunch of bullshit when he said he didn't have an address for her. I'll get her address. I don't think the bartender would want a marked unit driving through his parking lot most of the night. It'd be bad for business. You know he's getting a cut. Hard to give up money you're used to getting for doing nothing."

"How much will this hurt John?" Sarah asked Hickman.

"Although it's two separate incidents technically, they're intertwined," he answered. "The news will play it up. The mayor and chief won't like it, but, hell, they're not on John's side anyway. Something smells here. I'll get back with Wilson. He's a good detective. I'll give him my thoughts on the matter. If we can get to the girl, we may turn something."

Hickman looked at me sternly and said, "Stay the hell away from the bar! Next time, you might not be so lucky. You're wife's too young to be widowed."

I could feel myself blushing again as Hickman stood to leave.

***

When I woke up Sunday morning, the alarm clock showed 9:00 o'clock. Sarah's side of the bed was empty. I took care of my daily routine before heading to the kitchen to make coffee. I usually make my own coffee because I like it strong enough to melt the mug off the handle. I guess it's an acquired taste from drinking strong coffee on late shift to stay alert. As I walked into the kitchen, the aroma of perked coffee filled the air. A note was taped to the cabinet above the coffee maker.

It was from Sarah. She had taken Amy and gone to church. I can't remember the last time I'd been in a church. We went to church when we were first married, but I slowly drifted away. I always had an excuse that was job related. I'd get in late and be too tired to get up. Sarah never stopped going. As I poured a mug of coffee, I made the resolution to start back. I needed to balance my life. I needed to regain faith in people. Law enforcement tends to make officers skeptical of people. You begin to look for ulterior motives in daily conversations. The behavior erodes relationships.

The Sunday edition of our local newspaper was on the kitchen table. It was thick with ads as usual. I like to look at the ads more than read the paper. Pulling a chair out to sit at the table, a picture on the front page caught my eye. It was me with my tee shirt pulled over my head. It was taken when I was changing shirts at my car. The headlines screamed: OFFICER INVOLVED IN SECOND SHOOTING INCIDENT. My stomach soured when I read the headlines.

I sat the mug next to the paper scanning the article. The article was all fluff with the exception of questioning why I was at the bar and why somebody would shoot at me. It insinuated there was more to the story than the police were willing to divulge. From what I read, the information given to the press was factual and complete. Law enforcement doesn't speculate publicly.

I flipped though the ads looking for lumber supplies. Before we separated, I had promised Sarah I would build a deck at the back of the house but had put it off for lack of time and funds. It looked like I was going to have plenty of spare time while I waited for the investigation to be completed. If the investigation turned south, I might have too much spare time and zero money. I might be looking for another job. I pushed that thought out of my mind gathering a sheet of paper to make a list of building supplies. Hammering nails would be therapeutic. I could take my frustration out on the nails. I'd put the material on my charge card and figure out how to pay for it later.

By the time Sarah and Amy got home, I had a rough list of boards, nails and concrete. Sarah had read the article before leaving for church. She wasn't upset about it. She thought it might swing some sympathy towards me. She asked if I could remember anybody I had arrested that might hold a grudge. I thought about people I had arrested. There were a few I considered potentially very dangerous.

Most police departments require an officer to be armed 24/7. There's a good reason for this policy. If a violent crime is committed in front of the officer while off duty, the officer has the means to react. The officer seldom knows the mental stability of the arrested offender. The officer may run into the offender in public while off duty and need a weapon for defense. Most departments would rather an off duty officer be a good witness unless the crime was a life and death situation. I didn't have my weapon when I needed it because of my suspension. I was used to the weapon's weight on my hip. I felt naked without it.

We took a walk with Amy in the stroller. Neighbors, who were outside enjoying the weather, waved at us as we passed. It may have been artificial, but my family was temporarily at peace. I had something on my mind, and I didn't think Sarah was going to agree with me. I didn't want to argue with her. "Sarah," I said. "I need to pay my respect to the widow of the officer who was killed. It's something I have to do. I'll go at the end of visitation hours. I don't know if she'll be receptive, but I have to go."

"No," Sarah responded not looking at me. "We have to go. It might be awkward, even embarrassing according to how she reacts, but it's the proper thing to do. I'll see if my mother will watch Amy."

***

We arrived at the funeral home at a quarter till eight in the evening. I was surprised to see the parking lot full of cars – many of them with light bars. The police department, which obviously was the chief and mayor, decided Frank was not officially killed in the line of duty. Therefore he wasn't entitled to the ceremony normally given. The rank and file viewed it differently. The brothers and sisters would honor their dead regardless of what the decision makers thought.

When Sarah and I entered the hall leading to the parlor with Frank's body, it was crowded with uniforms, not all of the same color or style. There was a multitude of different badges. All the badges had a thin black ribbon stretched diagonally across signifying the lost of a fellow officer. Not all of the officers knew Frank personally. They were there to honor a fallen brother. There were brown uniforms of deputy sheriffs, various styles of blue uniforms from other police departments, grey uniforms of the state police and green uniforms of conservation officers.

I was dressed in a dark blue suit, white button down shirt and black tie. I didn't have a badge to clip onto my suit. Sarah wore a simple black dress without a necklace. She tightly held onto my hand as I threaded through the maze of officers. I spotted an older woman dressed in a dark blue dress attended by two young women standing next to Frank's coffin. Her face was puffy. She had been crying.

As we walked towards her, she stared at me with a puzzled look. When I stopped about two feet from her, Sarah moved beside me. Grey was winning the battle overtaking the woman's brown hair. Her eyes were lifeless as if her spirit were broken. Her dress was beginning to fray around the cuffs. I thought I saw a flicker of recognition in her eyes.

"Mrs. Glass?" I asked.

"Yes," she answered. There were a few seconds of silence which seemed like an eternity before she asked with a slight slur, "You're the officer who was with Frank when he was killed?"

"Yes ma'am," I answered. "This is my wife, Sarah."

The woman's eyes glanced to Sarah and then locked back onto me. "I'm very sorry about Frank…"

She interrupted me stepping very close to my face, "I thought I recognized you from the pictures in the newspaper. I have a question for you. Who was Frank fucking this time?"

I felt my face turn scarlet. The two younger women looked very embarrassed as they moved beside the widow taking hold of her arms. I felt Sarah slip an arm around mine. "I can't honestly say I know the answer," I stuttered.

Frank's widow looked like she was about to explode as one of the young women moved between us gently turning her around with the help of the other woman. Sarah pulled me towards the exit. Faces were staring at us. Obviously, they had heard the exchange. I looked at the floor as Sarah guided me out of the funeral home.

We were silent as we walked towards our car. Out of the shadows appeared the younger woman who had stepped in front of a widow. She was in her early twenties. Unlike the widow, she was well dressed. Something about her physical features told me she was related to Frank. She quickly intercepted us before we reached the car.

She was the first to speak, "I'm Frank Glass' daughter, Cynthia. Mom's not normally like this. She's been drinking. Dad…."

She paused as if trying to decide what to say, "Well, Dad was Dad. He liked the ladies. Mom knew he would never change, but she wouldn't leave him. Dad was never home. He was always working, yet there was never any money. I'm ashamed to say that I'm relieved it's over. Dad had enough time to retire. I hope Mom can draw his pension."

She looked chagrined realizing she had spoken too freely, "It's not your fault what happened to Dad. I apologize for my mother's behavior. Thank you for coming."

Her eyes were glistening with tears forming as she abruptly turned walking back into the shadows. Sarah nudged me towards our car as she said, "Listen to her. Frank's death is not your fault. You did the right thing. You paid your respect to his family."

CHAPTER 6

Monday morning I got up with Sarah to see her off to work. I was on child duty with Amy. I admit I wasn't as adept as Sarah when it came to feeding Amy. Amy was more interested in playing with her breakfast than eating it. There was only one solution for the breakfast catastrophe – a change of clothes and bath for Amy. The toddler enjoyed splashing as I kneeled by the tub gently sponging her clean. I was soaked by the end of her bath. I dressed her and placed her in the playpen with a few toys.

I started to fix breakfast for myself when the doorbell rang. It was the postman with a letter I had to sign for. It was from the police department. I ripped the envelope open quickly reading the contents. It was formal and straight to the point. On Wednesday, I was to report to headquarters at 10:00 A.M. to be interviewed a second time by homicide. It stated I had the right to be represented by an attorney. I decided to call Henry Fellows.

To my surprise and relief, I was put straight through to Fellows. I explained to him about the letter. He didn't seem awed. Fellows asked, "We need to meet an hour before you give your interview. I'm curious about Saturday night although I suspect there's little you can add to what I've been informed by William. I've been going over my notes from our last conversation."

He paused as if deciding whether to ask this question or not. Finally he asked, "Did you know prostitutes conducted business in the bar?"

I was embarrassed to answer, "I suspected there was prostitution going on, but I did not witness any exchange of money or physical activity."

Again there was a pause before Fellows said, "If this subject is brought up during the session, as your attorney, I advise to answer "no". Suspecting and knowing are two different things. If you are asked about a suspicion of prostitution on the premises, let me handle the question."

Fellows' statement reminded me about the legality concerning probable cause. Just because a police officer suspected a person had committed a crime, it couldn't be considered enough evidence to get a search warrant or make an arrest. Suspicion wasn't evidence. Suspicion couldn't be introduced in court. A person's rights are protected by the fourth amendment. A police officer is afforded the same protection.

As if he were a teacher instructing a student, Fellows continued, "John, I'm not advising you to lie. Answer the questions factually. The law is very technical. You're not lying by omission. You did not… I repeat myself, not know for certain prostitution was taking place. You're a trained officer. Through observation, your suspicion may be aroused which may prompt you to investigate. In this instance, you did not investigate."

Fellows told me to dress in a suit for the statement. He'd drive me to headquarters. He expected the press to be present. He instructed me to let him handle any questions from the reporters. Closing the conversation, he said, "This is a hot potato that the mayor and the chief are going to want to drop immediately. Expect the DA to be present. This is not a routine homicide investigation. You can believe there's a lot of political pressure. They just want it to go away."

After we disconnected, I thought about his parting statement. I felt like the mayor and the chief were willing to sacrifice me in order get on with the mayor's re-election campaign. I was a liability. Liabilities are to be shed during an election year.

***

I decided to keep busy Tuesday. I arranged for my mom to watch Amy while I shopped for deck supplies. Mom stole Amy from my arms disappearing into the house. I heard Amy laughing with delight. Dad, who's retired, came out the side door with his keys in hand. He had a smile on his face as he asked, "Want some help? We can take the pickup truck. It'll save you the delivery cost."

I nodded my head and backed my car out of the driveway parking it in front of the house. Dad pulled the truck beside my car stopping for me to get in. I was hesitant to start a conversation. I didn't want any more conflict. I had enough on my plate and didn't want a lecture from Dad. Looking at him, it hit me that Dad was no longer the young man I always pictured in my mind.

He was an older man who was amazingly in good physical shape after a lifetime of hard manual labor. Although his face showed age, he had the spry movement of a much younger man. There wasn't an ounce of excess fat on his frame. I felt ashamed for not spending more time with him. Time is a finite value. When we've used up our share, we're gone. I couldn't go backwards in time to make amends with him, but I could accept the olive branch he was extending. Clearing my throat, I said, "I don't know how the shooting is going to come out."

There was a long silence before he spoke, "I've been doing a lot of thinking lately. John, I've voiced my opinion about you being a police officer too often. I've been wrong... for all the right reasons. It wasn't about the pay. I was worried about you being hurt or killed. You work all kinds of shifts, and it's hard to have a family life. When all this happened, I realized it was your life. You chose a profession which gave you satisfaction. Hell, I guess if life was all about money, I would have done something else and not worked with my hands."

I was shocked. Dad was a man who never backed up once he had made a decision. I thought of him as an oak tree that would rather break than bend with the wind. I was wrong. Dad kept his eyes on the road not even glancing at me. It took a lot for him to make this admission. Watching him, I said, "I like being a cop, but now I'm not too sure I made the correct choice. It's caused troubles between me and Sarah. I don't know if I'll even have a job when it's over."

"Everybody has bumps in the road in marriage," he answered. "Even your mom and I have had our differences. You were too young to remember. It was mostly my fault. Had to get my head on straight – priorities. I didn't have the right priorities. Won't matter if they fire you in the long scheme of things. What matters is family. It took me too long to figure that out. I think you've figured it out for yourself."

We discussed the shooting as he drove to the lumber yard. I wasn't worried about Dad talking about it. He wasn't the type to talk about personal matters to anybody. As a matter of fact, he wasn't the type to talk much at all. This was probably the longest conversation I had ever had with him.

The rest of the afternoon passed in relative silence. Although we worked side by side, little conversation was exchanged. I enjoyed being with him. I truly can't explain, but it was as if some of his strength and determination passed into me. I had my family.

***

When Sarah came home, I hoisted Amy onto my hip and took Sarah to survey the stack of lumber in the back yard. She seemed surprised when I told her Dad was going to help build the deck. She arched in eyebrow but didn't question me. I bathed Amy while she prepared dinner. It was a good division of labor. I was better at cleaning than cooking. I dressed Amy and carried her into the kitchen placing her on the floor with a play set. Sarah was standing in front of the stove stirring spaghetti sauce while the noodles boiled.

I got a spoon out of the utensil drawer with the intention of tasting the sauce. I was starved. I stood beside Sarah with my back towards the kitchen windows. Sarah pretended to slap my hand as I reached for the bubbling sauce. Amy had crawled in front of me pulling herself up using my legs. As I spooned a mouthful of sauce, the living room windows exploded. The kitchen widows exploded showering the room with shards of glass. I grabbed Sarah dragging her onto the floor. I covered Amy with by body.

I could feel splinters of glass imbedded in my back. Sarah was crying out in pain. She was lying on her back holding the upper section of her left arm. The sleeve of her white blouse was scarlet red. Blood was seeping through her fingers. Images of Frank flashed into my mind. My God! Please don't let me lose Sarah!

The rapid firing of a fully automatic weapon from outside ceased with the loud squealing of tires as a vehicle accelerated. I leaped to my feet clutching Amy to my chest. I felt like my heart was going to explode in my chest as I ran to our bedroom quickly putting Amy in her playpen. I ripped a bath towel from its holder and ran back to Sarah.

She was laying in the floor sobbing. I had to pry her hand off of the wound wrapping the towel tightly around her arm. Cradling her head in my arms, I rocked her unable to speak. Sirens were wailing in the background as the police responded to the neighbors' 911 calls. I could hear tires screeching as the police cars stopped in front of the house.

We had left the front door unlocked. I heard it slam open. An officer appeared in the kitchen doorway with his weapon drawn and pointing at me. "My wife has been shot! Get an ambulance!" I shouted.

A second officer appeared behind the first officer. He holstered his weapon immediately keying his portable radio's mic asking for an E.M.S. unit. The first officer holstered his pistol staring at my back. It was bloody from the glass puncture wounds. I could hear other officers moving through the house clearing rooms. An officer yelled, "There's a child back here!"

Sarah was struggling to get up, crying, "Amy! I have to see her! Is she all right?"

I held Sarah in my arms shouting to the officer, "She's our daughter! Please check to see if she is OK!"

Within a minute, another officer was in the kitchen doorway. He said, "Your child looks OK. I left her in the playpen. I don't think she should see this. She has a few cuts, but I don't think it's anything serious. I think it'd be wise to have E.M.S. take a look."

A young man carrying a large orange colored medical bag accompanied by a woman came into the kitchen. Without speaking, they put on blue vinyl gloves. The man gently pried Sarah from my arms while the woman helped me to my feet. Two more E.M.T.s entered the kitchen carrying a gurney. The kitchen was crowded with bodies. I was guided to the living room by the woman. All but one police officer followed us.

I heard one of the E.M.T's say, "It looks worse than it is. A bullet grazed her arm. There's a lot of bleeding though. Better start an IV and get some fluid in her to be on the safe side."

The E.M.T.s were efficient. While one put a pressure dressing on Sarah's arm, the two others slid a spine board underneath her quickly strapping her onto the board. Two lifted her using the board onto the gurney before raising it. As they rolled Sarah into the living room, she looked at me crying out, "I want to see Amy! I want my baby!"

I broke away from the woman running to Sarah. I grasped her hand, "She's OK. You need to go to the hospital. I'll take care of Amy."

As they rolled Sarah out of the house, I became enraged. I was beyond anger! You may try to kill me but leave my family alone! I saw a look of recognition on the face of one of the officers. He asked, "You're John Drake?"

"Yes sir," I answered.

"What the hell happened?" he asked.

"I don't know," I replied. "It looks like a drive-by shooting. Maybe the gang members of the guy I shot."

The other officers instantly made the connection. Their body language conveyed the same anger that I felt. Only the lowest vermin would hurt an officer's family. Whoever had done this had broken the rules. There would be no holds barred in apprehending these criminals. I heard one of the officers mumble under his breath, "Motherfuckers!"

The woman E.M.T. took my arm to get my attention, "We need you take you to the hospital. You've got a lot of glass in your back. You need a doctor to take a look at it."

"I have to get somebody to watch Amy," I answered in a panic. "I'll call my folks."

"Make the call. Give me their address, and I'll take her to them," offered an officer.

I examined Amy assuring myself she wasn't hurt. I found a few superficial scratches on her face, nothing serious. I made the call. Mom answered the phone. I told her Sarah had been hurt. A police officer was bringing Amy for her to watch while I went to the hospital. I know she wanted to know more, but I didn't have time to answer any questions. I'd explain what happened later. Because of the fragments of glass protruding out of my back, the E.M.T.s decided the prudent thing was for me to lie on my stomach on the gurney. I didn't think I needed to be on a gurney, but they insisted.

The ride to University Hospital was not pleasant. I don't know what I expected. Either the ambulance was built without shock absorbers, or the driver went out of his way to hit every bump or pothole. I have to admit that I wasn't in the best frame of mind. The pain in my back intensified.

My adrenaline charge was wearing off. Even my butt and thighs started complaining. I must have taken some glass there.

At the hospital, I asked for Sarah. I wasn't sure we were at the same hospital. The triage nurse told me Sarah was there. She informed me that Sarah was in stable condition. Whether it was intentional or by accident, I was taken to a room next to Sarah. They were not conventional rooms, rather a large area separated by curtains giving the image of separate rooms.

A female nurse dressed in olive green scrubs came to my bedside. It was difficult to see what she looked like being I was lying face down. The nurse said that Sarah was asking for me. She asked me if I'd like to be able to see my wife. It didn't make sense to me that she'd have to ask. Probably some hospital rule about privacy. Naturally I said yes. The nurse pulled back the curtain separating Sarah and me.

I shifted a little to my side so I could see her. The back of Sarah's bed was elevated about 45 degrees. She was in a hospital gown with a white sheet pulled up to her waist. I could see a dressing wrapped around the area where she had been shot. Sarah looked at me with her eyes glassy with tears. "Is Amy OK?"

"She has a few scratches. She's at my folks," I assured her and asked, "How's the arm?"

"I'm OK. My arm smarts a little," she answered. "The doctor said a bullet nicked me. It took off a layer of skin. He said another quarter of an inch, and it'd missed my arm completely. What about you?"

"I know how pin cushions feel," I quipped trying to lighten the situation for Sarah's sake.

A young man in surgical scrubs came into my room. He was carrying a metal tray stacked with instruments and gauze. He curtly closed the curtain separating Sarah and me. He introduced himself as a doctor. He didn't look old enough to be a doctor. He looked like a teenager. Then again, maybe I'm getting old.

He retrieved a large pair of scissors from the tray cutting the back of my shirt up the center. He informed me that he didn't want to remove the shirt by pulling it over my head because of all the glass embedded in my back. When he peeled the shirt off, I understood what he meant. Damn it hurt! Two more skillful cuts with the scissors removed the bulk of my shirt.

He used the same procedure for my pants and underwear. I have to give him credit for salvaging my belt. One point for the doctor. He opted not to numb my back and other unmentionable parts of my body because it was such a large area. Minus one point for the doctor. It took forever to remove all the fragments. A most unpleasant experience. After he was finished, he painted my backside. I think it was iodine. It burned like hell!

Having finished, the boy doctor told me that there wasn't major damage, and I'd be sore for a few days. He said I'd remember what happened every time I sat, at least for a few days. I believe he was trying to make a joke. I didn't think it was funny. He asked me if I needed anything for pain. I refused. The doctor covered me with a sheet before pulling back the curtain that separated Sarah and me. He nodded at Sarah as he left.

A short time later, Detective Wilson was at my bedside. After inquiring how I was, he spoke to Sarah. I could tell he was trying to control his anger about what had happened. He returned to my bed shaking his head as he said, "There are 9 mm casings all over the road by your house. I'm requesting a marked unit to sit on your house until we can figure this thing out.

"When I left, the crime scene technicians were digging bullets out of the walls. Some of the bullets penetrated the interior walls into the bedrooms. Other detectives are canvassing the neighborhood for witnesses. I don't know if both of you will be released, but I'd strongly suggest staying someplace else tonight if you are."

He paused and lowered his voice before asking, "John, you have your concealed carry deadly weapons permit?"

Police Officers are issued them free. All the officer had to do was apply. Most officers had them because some states didn't honor an out of state badge when an officer was carrying, but they did honor a CCDW permit. Laws differ from state to state. I answered in the affirmative.

"You have a personal off duty weapon?" Wilson asked.

"I have a Glock model 27," I answered.

"As a friend, I'd advise carrying it. You may be suspended, but you still have rights as a citizen. I'm perplexed about the whole situation. There have been two attempts on your life in two days. Both attempts are so different that I can't make a connection. I don't believe either of them are random acts. The first attempt was more like an individual action. The second attempt was like a gang drive-by. Perhaps a gangbanger failed the first time and got his buddies to help the second time. I don't think that's the case. When I leave here, I'm going to contact the gang unit. I think it's time to put pressure on the bastards! Start calling in chips. If we put enough pressure on them, somebody will talk."

Shortly after Wilson left, my dad arrived. His face was drawn. The man was tired. The officer had delivered Amy to their house as promised. The officer only gave my folks sketchy details because he said it was an ongoing investigation. In actuality, I don't think the officer knew more than what he told them. Dad didn't press for any details. He knew that we'd discuss them later. He was more concerned about our physical condition.

CHAPTER 7

Sarah and I were discharged from the hospital close to midnight. Both of us were given prescriptions for antibiotics and pain along with a sheath of instructions. The hospital gave me blue scrubs that felt like they were made from a thick woven paper material. Sarah wore an identical blue scrub top. Her slacks hadn't been cut off. Our bloody clothes had been put in a paper bag which Wilson took for evidence. Sarcasm sometimes creeps into my thought process. The clothes would only be good for evidence if they caught the culprits who did this.

It was decided that we'd spend the night at my folks. Dad had his car parked on the street close to the ER. Again sarcasm entered my mind. I didn't think that I could turn a drive-by shooting into my insurance company as a claim.

Then a feeling of helplessness and despair overtook me. I had no police powers. Now I'd have to depend upon my law enforcement brothers and sisters for protection. We were depending on Sarah's income. She was hurt. We didn't have much saved. We'd quickly exhaust our savings. I pushed the depressing thoughts from my mind. I'd address them tomorrow when I could think clearly.

As we exited the ER, I saw a Channel 12 news van parked at the curb across from the ER. Jacob Bellows jumped out of the van as we walked towards Dad's car. Didn't this guy ever sleep? We picked up our pace as Bellows trotted towards us. His camera man struggled to keep up with him. This was not going to be pleasant!

Sarah was safely in the back seat of the car when Bellows reached us. He shoved a microphone at me loudly asking, "Why is somebody trying to kill you? Do you know who it is?"

The camera's lights were blinding. Dad roughly shouldered his way between us wrapping an arm around me. Dad maneuvered to keep Bellows at arm's length as he guided me into the front passenger seat. It took all of my will not to verbally lash out at Bellows. If I knew who was trying to kill me, wouldn't the police have arrested them? He was an idiot! No, he was baiting me. It was a calculated ploy to make me look out of control. He hadn't changed his tactic.

I was out of Bellow's reach in the car. He started badgering Dad with questions. Who are you? What do you know about the shooting? How bad were the Drakes injured? Bellows stopped asking questions taking a step backwards. I swear... I saw my dad's face transform. It was a face I have never seen before. It was... The only way I could describe it would be the cold face of death. Without uttering a word, Dad got into the car.

Driving the car away from the curb, Dad said, "I almost lost it back there."

He became silent. He was in deep thought. Both Sarah and I sensed it was not the time to interrupt with questions. There was a sadness in his voice when he resumed talking, "Before both of you were born, there was a great injustice done to the soldiers returning from an unpopular war. I'm not saying it was a just or unjust war. Soldiers don't make policy. Politicians, civilians, make policy. Soldiers are given orders to do their country's bidding.

"I'm saying the returning soldiers were not treated with the respect they deserved. Some of the soldiers were spit on and called baby killers. Others were cursed openly in public. The My Lai Massacre was all over the news. My Lai was horrible. Innocent civilians were slaughtered, but it was a crime committed by a few men. The news became so focused on My Lai that the public began viewing soldiers as randomly killing women and children.

"It was a difficult war. The enemy was not always in uniform. Women walked up to soldiers and killed them. At times, the soldiers didn't know who the enemy was. Mistakes were made. It's hard to judge unless you were there in the heat of action. The public forgot how many lives were sacrificed in service to their country. I blame the media for much of the

61

way the soldiers were viewed at home because of how they were presented in the news. It was about political viewpoints and ratings.

"The point I'm trying to make is that I see a parallel in this situation. I think this reporter has an agenda. I've seen his editorials on the news. You were thrust into a terrible situation that required you to take action. He's Monday morning quarterbacking. He's out to hang you while making a name for him and increasing the station's viewership."

Dad changed the subject suggesting that he and I go to an all night pharmacy after dropping Sarah off at the folk's house. He had briefly opened the door into his past. Now the door was closed again and locked. I knew he had been in the army during the Vietnam era, but he never talked about it. In his book of life, it was a chapter he preferred to remain closed.

The kitchen and living room lights were on when we arrived. Mom came out as Dad parked the car. She hugged Sarah and me. Sarah went to Amy's crib finding our daughter sleeping soundly. When Sarah returned to the kitchen, Mom fussed over her insisting on making her some hot cocoa. Dad told Mom that we were going to get the prescriptions filled. Sarah started filling her in on what happened as he nudged me towards the door.

As Dad backed the car out of the driveway, I said, "I need to go by our house and get some clothes. I have a meeting at headquarters in the morning. My attorney is going with me."

"OK," he answered. "Probably a good idea to turn off the furnace. Can't keep the heat inside with broken windows. It's not cold enough weather to freeze the pipes."

***

There was a patrol car parked in front of the house. When Dad pulled into the driveway, the marked unit's spotlight came on illuminating Dad's car. I got out of the car using my hand to shield my eyes from the blinding light. Wearing the paper scrubs, I couldn't appear as much of a threat. The officer turned off the spotlight. A small yellow glow remained in the center of the spotlight as the filament cooled. I could barely make out the outline of the driver's door opening.

I saw an object in the officer's hand. I immediately raised both hands to show I wasn't armed. It was obviously a flashlight when the officer turned it on. He stopped six feet from me. I could see a piece of paper in his other hand. His eyes flicked between the paper and my face as he asked, "Who are you?"

"I'm John Drake. I live here," I answered.

"Just double checking," he said. "I've got a photo copy of your picture. It actually looks like you. Who's in the car?"

"My dad, we came by to get some clothes. My family and I are spending the night at my parents' house," I said.

"Good idea," he commented.

Dad had a flashlight turned on as he walked around the front of the car. I don't know where he got it, but it seemed he was always prepared. His flashlight's beam danced across the front of the house. The house looked like a picture from a war zone. It was something you'd expect to see in Bosnia. All the front windows were shattered. There was a random pattern where bullets had pockmarked the bricks.

I could hear glass crunching under my shoes. I fumbled for the wall switch. When I turned the lights on, I became nauseous. A thousand pieces of glass sparkled on the floor. There were holes in the interior walls from bullets passing through the windows. Pools of semi dried blood were on the kitchen floor. The officer stood beside Dad shaking his head. Dad didn't say anything, but I could see anger in his face.

I went to the master bedroom closet taking the largest suitcase from the closet. Bullets had passed through the interior walls and living space. On the exterior walls, I saw where the CSI technicians had dug out bullets that had lodged into the brick. I gathered clothes that I thought Sarah and I would need and dumped them into the suitcase. Then I went to Amy's room. Turning on the light in her bedroom, I realized how narrowly we had escaped tragedy.

Amy's crib was positioned against the interior wall of the room. One of the wooden rails of the crib was broken where a bullet struck it. The bullet had passed two inches above the mattress where we routinely laid Amy. If she had been in the crib, the bullet would have killed her. I don't know how to express my mixed emotions. I was both angry and thankful at the same time. I was thankful that none of us were killed. I was angry at the animals that committed such a heinous act.

I heard the furnace stop running. Dad had found the thermostat. I scooped a few things from Amy's dresser tossing them into the suitcase. I felt like I was going to explode with anger. I wanted out of the room. I zipped the suitcase close and rapidly left the room going to the living room. Dad and the police officer stopped talking when I entered.

The officer extended his hand saying, "John, I'm Henry Platt. I don't know how long they'll pay for us to sit on your house, but I'm willing do it without pay on my days off. I'll talk to the guys at the office. I think that I can get enough volunteers to cover your house for a few weeks when they pull us off."

I pumped Officer Platt's hand in gratitude. There was no way I could express how much his willingness to sacrifice his time from his family in order to protect my family meant to me. I heard anger in his voice when he said, "We can't let the bastards get away with this! It could have been my family or another officer's family!"

We turned all the lights out and locked the front door before leaving. I pitched the suitcase in the back seat as Dad got in the driver's side. On the way to the pharmacy, Dad said, "In the morning, I'll get some plywood to cover the windows while you're downtown. It'll be a temporary fix until we can locate the glass panes."

"When I'm finished downtown, I'll help," I answered.

***

I hate the beeping sound from an alarm clock. Perhaps it's because it disrupts the natural sleep pattern. The human body knows when it's had enough sleep. Enough of my tirade about alarm clocks. I turned over glaring at the clock, not that the clock cared, before slapping at it until it stopped the incessant beeping. As my mind finally started functioning, I realized that Sarah wasn't in bed. I'm not a morning person. It takes a moment for people like me to function.

My body protested as I sat up on the side of the bed. My body was stiff and sore. I felt like I had taken a beating. My body was reminding me of the trauma from yesterday. I turned on the bedside lamp almost knocking it off the stand. Fumbling around in the suitcase, I retrieved a tee shirt slowly pulling it over my head. My back smarted as the soft cloth slid over it. I slipped on the paper scrub pants.

Doing a slow shuffle to the kitchen, I saw Sarah and Mom at the table drinking coffee. Sarah was wearing jeans and a blouse. I remembered getting a pair of jeans last night, but I didn't remember packing the blouse.

64

It had to be Mom's. The shoes were the same ones she had on last night. The bulky dressing from the hospital was replaced with two small gauze pads taped on her arm.

She smiled at me and said, "I was going to give you a few minutes. I thought you may have turned the alarm off and went back to sleep."

"How are you feeling?" I asked.

"It hurts a little, but I've had worse. Remember, I've had a baby," she quipped.

I was concerned. She had just gone through a traumatic experience, not only physically but psychologically.

"I'm going to take the day off," she answered. "I need some time to settle down. I'm going to spend the day with Amy and your Mom. If you can get the windows repaired, Amy and I will come home tonight."

"Don't you think it'd be wise to stay here a couple of nights?" I asked.

She ignored my question. She said, "John, we can't stop living and hide. That's what they want. They want to intimidate. That's not going to happen! Besides, I need to work. We need the money. Your mom is lending me her car. Eat breakfast, get dressed. I'll drop you off by our house so you can get your car."

I knew that no matter what argument I presented Sarah wouldn't listen. My best course of action was to follow instructions. Dad had already left to gather supplies to repair the windows. He left word that he'd be at our house when I finished downtown.

***

I was in Henry Fellows' office by eight. As before, he was dressed in an expensive suit. He had a thick folder open lying on the desk in front of him. I saw newspaper clippings about the drive by shooting on top of other clippings. A stack of typed papers and yellow pages from a legal tablet were below the clippings. He had been perusing the file before I arrived.

There was genuine concern in his voice as he asked, "How is Sarah?"

"She's having some pain. She's taking the day off from work," I answered figuring he had read that she had been wounded.

"My mother always said women could take more pain than men," he commented before asking about me and Amy.

After I informed him about our conditions, Fellows said, "You can expect the investigators to ask questions about the attempts on your life and the attempt on your family's life. It's logical that they're intertwined. Don't take affront at the questions I'm going to ask you. As your attorney, I have to know the truth even if I don't like what I hear. Are you involved in any activity that would or could cause the attempts on your life?"

I was insulted by the question. How dare Fellows thinking I was involved in some kind of criminal activity! Then I thought about what he had said. Don't take affront at the questions. As my attorney, he couldn't divulge my answers. He was preparing for the interrogation. He didn't want to be caught off guard. Or, he was preparing me.

"I'm not nor have ever have participated in any criminal activity," I answered looking him in the eyes. "I have no idea why I was shot at the first time. I suspect but don't know for sure that the drive by shooting was gang related. The man I shot was a gang member."

Fellows continued to pepper me with questions taking copious notes. Sometimes he'd pause advising me to answer in a different manner. He wasn't advising me to lie. I sensed he thought selective details of the interrogation would be leaked to the press. I believe he was concerned about how the information could be portrayed to manipulate the public although he never addressed it openly.

To say that I was uncomfortable going to homicide was an understatement. Fellows drove us to police headquarters in his Mercedes. The smell of leather permeated the interior. I thought about his car as we rode in silence. The car had to cost more than I made in a year. I'd never be able to afford a Mercedes. I'd never be able to give my family the standard of living that Fellows had.

He parked in a pay lot a block from headquarters. News trucks with their telescoping antennas extended were clustered around headquarters. The sharks had gathered for the blood feast. Fellows set a brisk pace as we approached the pack of reporters. They started shouting questions before we reached them. Fellows stopped, raising a hand to stop the questions. He made one statement, "My client has nothing to say at this time."

Headquarters was an old seven story brick building adjacent to city hall. A major was waiting for us in the lobby as we entered. The major was impeccably dressed. I couldn't see a wrinkle or piece of lint on his dark blue uniform. After a quick introduction, he led us to a small conference room equipped with audio visual recording devices. The DA was sitting at the table with a Styrofoam cup of coffee. He rose and shook Fellows hand. He didn't offer his hand to me.

The DA was a short thin man named James Durbin. His hair, the few strands visible, was carefully plastered in place in an attempt to cover his receding hairline. The back of his shoulders were rounded in a hump. I assumed it was from sitting and leaning over a desk. Thick black framed glasses resting on a nose that resembled a vulture's beak hid tiny black eyes. His nose was the dominate feature of his face. It wouldn't take a large imagination to see him as a vulture, just add a few feathers. His black suit didn't help.

The major informed us that he would be conducting the interview. Major is an appointed position, not a merit position. He was part of the upper command and had been handpicked for the interview. He was part of the chief's team. He understood the chief's and mayor's agendas. I knew other officers and, perhaps, the chief would be watching the interview from another location. Everything would be recorded.

The major didn't read me Miranda because my attorney was present. I gave the pertinent information such as my name, rank, badge number and assignment. With the first question, I knew I was in trouble. Locking eyes with me, the major asked, "Officer Drake, did you submit the form requesting permission to work off duty at the Double H Lounge?"

"No, sir," I answered. "I thought Frank had taken care of it. He's worked there many times."

"You're referring to Officer Frank Glass?"

"Yes sir."

"You have been issued a manual of our policy and procedures, have you not?" he asked.

"Yes sir."

"Have you read them as required?"

The DA had a sly grin. The major had been coached. I was being led into a carefully constructed trap. They knew I had a copy. I had to sign for the manual when I received it. I felt my guts twisting into a knot. I hesitated before answering, "I have glanced over them, but I haven't read the manual."

The major kept his face expressionless; however, the DA's face had an expression that said "Got you!" Fellows remained mute scribbling a few notes on a yellow legal pad. The major continue along the same line of questioning, "Were you aware that each officer is responsible for submitting a permission request to work off duty?"

He had me. I looked at Fellows for help. Fellows whispered in my ear, "Go ahead and answer him truthfully."

"Yes sir, I suppose I did, but I didn't think of it," I answered watching the DA smirking at my response.

The major's next question got Fellows' attention, "Did you know prostitutes were working at the bar?"

"No sir," I quickly answered.

"Surely, as a trained police officer, you suspected something?" he asked sarcastically.

Fellows loudly interrupted, "Major, with all due respect, I object to the question! As an officer, you know that a suspicion cannot be introduced as evidence in a court of law. An officer can suspect, but that's all it is – not fact. We are here to give factual information not conjecture."

Anger flashed across the major's face. He moved his eyes to the DA questioning whether to push the point of or to move to the next question. The DA drummed his fingers on the table before speaking, "You're objection is noted, councilor. However, I believe there is pertinence to the question. Please have your client answer the question."

Fellows and I had discussed this question before hand. I answered as Fellows had advised, "I did not see any exchange of money or sexual acts. I can't say prostitution was taking place."

The major and DA appeared frustrated. Their trap had a hole in it. The DA snapped, "The major didn't ask if you saw prostitution! He asked if you suspected prostitution!"

"Whether he suspected or didn't suspect prostitution, it has no bearing on the facts of this inquiry! Mr. Drake was observant enough to note that no money exchanged hands, and he did not witness carnal acts," Fellows replied raising his voice.

"I think your client is skirting an important issue. I think he knows more than he's stating," the DA directed at Fellows. "Since the incident, the police have arrested several women at the bar for soliciting prostitution. Obviously, there was criminal activity taking place on the premises at the time of the incident. I question why an honest police officer would work at such an establishment and not comprehend what was going on? Why would there be two attempts on Drakes' life?"

"Think as you may! I'm positive if Mr. Drake knew who was trying to kill him, he would have informed the authorities. My understanding is this is a police investigation. To my knowledge, Mr. Drake has not been charged with a crime. Neither Mr. Drake nor I have received a subpoena from the DA's office for a deposition. I haven't objected to you being present as a courtesy. I strongly advise the major to move on with his questioning," retorted Fellows.

The two attorneys glared at each other waiting for the other to blink. Finally, the DA ordered the major, "Proceed Major."

Fellows had told me if I was pushed hard enough, I'd have to answer. He also thought if the DA were present, he would be hesitant to push too hard because technically it wasn't the DA's case. They had been opponents in other cases with Fellows consistently winning. Still, I questioned if I lied. I did suspect but didn't investigate. Was it a lie by omission?

The major frowned as he glanced at an open notebook lying on the table directly in front of him. I guessed it contained a list of questions to be asked. The major coughed lightly to clear his throat before asking, "Why did you go back to the bar after the incident? As an officer, didn't you think you would be interfering with an ongoing investigation?"

I cringed because I knew they were not going to like my response. I answered, "I don't know why I went back. I was driving, trying to recall what happened. I didn't plan on going to the bar. I didn't think about an investigation. It just happened."

"It just happened," repeated the major with more than a hint of doubt.

"How much were you paid," the major asked?

"I was supposed to get 30 dollars an hour. I refused the money," I answered.

I saw surprise in the faces of both the major and DA. The major fired back, "Why didn't you take the money?"

I knew they wouldn't understand, but I tried to express my feelings, "I didn't want it. It felt wrong to take money being Officer Glass was killed."

The interrogation lasted for another hour. The same questions were asked in different ways. I knew they were trying to catch me in a lie. If I were caught lying, it would cast doubt on my credibility. The credibility of a witness is important. It can make or break a case in court. My gut feeling told me that they were not interested in the truth. They were interested in hanging me out to dry.

CHAPTER 8

Fellows and I discussed my testimony as we drove back to his office. Several interesting facts were revealed. Only two empty shell casings were found at the scene. Both of the empty casings were from my weapon. Only one partially intact bullet was retrieved was from the drug dealer. It was from my weapon. Frank's femoral artery had been severed by a bullet causing him to bleed to death. There were no powder burns on Frank's clothing which indicated that he was not shot from a close proximity.

I asked Fellows about going to the funeral home the other day to pay my respects to Frank. Fellows preferred that I had not gone, but he understood. The police department was taking the stance that Frank's death was not in the line of duty because he was working off duty. Limited honors would be given to him during the funeral. Once again, the mayor and chief were distancing themselves from the incident.

Rather than taking me back to his office, Fellows dropped me off at my car. Luckily it started. The drive home was uneventful. Pulling into my driveway, I could see Dad had repaired one window and was working on a second window. As I headed towards him, he told me to go change clothes. He'd come into the house for lunch as soon as he had the pane of glass in place.

As I entered the house, I could smell wet plaster. Dad had patched the bullet holes. Partial cans of paint were stacked in the kitchen's corner. Obviously, Dad had found them in the garage. A 12 gauge Mossberg pump shotgun was in the corner. A box of buckshot was lying by the gun's stock. It was Dad's shotgun. I didn't comment.

Dad was scrubbing his hands in the kitchen sink by the time I had changed clothes. I told him about my testimony, and what I'd learned. Wrinkling his forehead in thought, he stated, "Doesn't sound like they have much to go on, but it they're up to something."

"Mr. Fellows thought the same thing," I answered. "They asked if I had an extra round loaded. I didn't. Some of the guys slide another round in the magazine after chambering a round. That gives them sixteen rounds. We're not supposed to do that."

"They're looking for the shot that killed the other police officer," he said. "If you'd had an extra round, they'd want to say you shot him. Still might try to say that."

I'd already thought about that scenario. They'd be presenting circumstantial evidence and drawing a conclusion from it. I've seen juries swayed by weaker evidence though. The DA would disregard any discrepancies. There was one known shooter – me. One bullet recovered – mine. No witnesses verifying a second shooter.

I couldn't prove I hadn't slipped an extra round into the magazine. A bystander could have picked up the empty shell casing as an explanation of why only two casings were found. Plus there was the fact that I was working at a bar where prostitution was taking place. I was being paid in cash. Would an honest cop put himself in this situation? Presented with the right spin, it could be damning.

"It's a wait and see situation," I answered. "It's their decision."

Dad told me about his morning activities during lunch. By dinnertime, we had repaired all the windows except the living room picture window. Dad thought he should spend the night at our house. I agreed with him. I wanted my family safe. To me, it was symbolically announcing that the thugs hadn't won. Their terror was not working.

After lunch, I helped Dad place a sheet of plywood on his saw horses. We would not be able to repair the picture window today so we were covering it with plywood. He took a quick measurement before using a power saw to cut it to the proper dimension.

I was glad Dad was spending the night. I realized what I had missed by isolating myself from him. I wanted to know the man. It was a relationship I had desired but was too stubborn to admit to myself. Now I was being honest with myself. Honesty is an absolute. My perspective had radically changed.

***

The house felt confining with the front window boarded. It felt like being in a cave. Dad had gone to get us KFC for dinner while I swept up the broken glass. I had dumped the last load of glass into the trash can and was mopping up the dried blood when Dad returned. He had two large bags of food. He sat the bags on the kitchen table removing two box suppers. Smiling, he said, "Got to take care of the troops. It wouldn't be right not to."

I got two cans of soft drink from the refrigerator for the officers outside. When I got to their car, they had the boxes opened and were chewing on the chicken. After thanking us, the driver said, "There's been a lot of talk among the ranks. The mayor hasn't supported us since he's been in office. We figure he's going to throw you under the bus. It's bullshit! The sons of bitches crossed the line when they shot up your home."

I thanked them for their support before returning to the house. When I turned on the television, there was a special news report with Bellows filling the screen. I turned up the volume to hear what he was saying. The picture showed Bellows in front of our house with all the police cars behind him.

He had a concerned expression as he said, "I have to question why a shooting of this nature would take place in a quiet residential neighborhood like this. Twice in two days Officer John Drake has been shot at. Why would somebody have such a compelling reason to try to either kill or intimidate Officer Drake? Now, not only is Drake's life in jeopardy, but his family's lives are in peril. As the saying goes, where there's smoke there's fire."

The television screen went black. Turning around, I saw Dad had the remote control in his hands. "I don't listen to ass holes."

That was an unusual statement for Dad. He seldom used profanity regardless of the situation. He continued, "He's walking a fine line. I'm not an attorney, but I think he's getting close to libel."

"I'm sure the station's got lawyers. He's run it by them before going on air," I responded.

73

"Don't be so sure," dad stated. "The big boys count on having more money than the average person. They figure they can bring bigger guns to court than you can afford. They're willing to absorb the legal costs if it increases the bottom line. Read about it with insurance companies. Deny a treatment and the person files suit. It drags out so long that the person dies from the illness. The case drops because a dead person can't sue. Same philosophy. The station wants ratings. They don't give a damn about your reputation or your life. That's a fact!"

I agreed with Dad that Bellows and the television station didn't care about what happened to me or my family. Hopefully, I had many years of life ahead. The outcome would determine the direction of my life. That was a fact!

***

Sarah arrived home with Amy at six in the evening. Dad and I were in the garage putting the last of our tools away. I got Amy out of her infant seat letting her ride on my hip while Dad pulled the garage door down. I had wanted to install an automatic garage door opener so Sarah could easily use the garage in foul weather, but money was always tight I didn't know how we were going to pay for the deck material. I had charged the material on my credit card. Not a wise move since I'd probably be unemployed shortly.

I could tell from her expression Sarah had something on her mind. "John, I had an interesting visitor today," she told me. I'll tell you about it once we're in the house. Perhaps you may want your father to hear this and get his input. He's good at reading situations."

I motioned for Dad to follow us into the house. Once we were inside, Sarah put Amy into her crib with a soft bodied doll and went to change into comfortable clothes. I started fixing a pot of decaffeinated coffee in our Mr. Coffee Machine. I think every family has certain routines. This was our routine before we had supper. Sarah and I would have coffee while talking about our day. At least this was our routine before I lost my bearing. It felt good. No, it felt right to be with family. I had my rudder back."

Dad busied himself washing his hands in the kitchen sink before getting three mugs out of the cabinet. I watched Dad as he carefully placed the mugs on the table. Each mug was centered before a chair with the mug's handle positioned facing right. He folded three paper napkins at a diagonal putting one by each mug with the point away from the mug once again on the right side. He noticed me watching commenting, "I'm getting pretty good at this domestic thing since I retired."

Sarah entered the kitchen dressed in an oversized tee shirt and well worn jeans. He face had a reddish hue from a fresh scrubbing. She seldom wore makeup at home which suited me just fine. I thought she was blessed with a complexion that didn't need any help from cosmetics. Of course, I realize my judgment is biased when it comes to her. Maybe something else had come into play. Maybe I had matured enough to realize Sarah's beauty came from the inner person – not from the structure housing her soul.

She went to Dad. She hugged him and buried her head into his chest. Dad looked somewhat embarrassed but said nothing. He's always been more of the strong silent type rather than the touchy feely type. Loosening her grip but not releasing him, Sarah looked up at Dad saying, "Thank you."

There was an awkward silence. I swear I actually think my dad blushed. He gently extracted himself from her arms guiding her to a chair. "You're family…" he said cocking his head to the side as if thinking about what to say. "Let me get the coffee, and we'll tell you what we accomplished today. Then you can tell us about your day."

***

After the coffee was poured, Sarah said, "Mark Mumford called the office today and asked for me to call him. He said it was important. The office called me on my cell phone with his message and phone number. At first, I wasn't going to talk to him, but I decided it wouldn't hurt to hear what he had to say. Mumford wouldn't talk over the phone.

I had him come to your folk's house because it would be private, out of public scrutiny. He had some very interesting information. Mumford said John is being investigated by Internal Affairs along with the homicide investigation. He wouldn't tell me his source, but I think the source is high up the police department's food chain and doesn't agree with the mayor or chief. They're building a case to fire John for breaking departmental policy among other things."

Dad didn't comment, but I knew the wheels were turning in his mind. It confirmed what I had suspected when I had been asked if I had sent the permission to work off duty form up the chain of command. Fellows said he hadn't objected although the question had nothing to do with the homicide investigation. If I were fired for breaking policy, Fellows believed he could have me re-instated by court order. He hadn't gone into detail.

Sarah took a slip of paper from her back pocket before continuing, "Mumford said the charge would be failure to have permission to work off duty. The department will take the stance that they wouldn't have allowed you to work at the bar because of prostitution taking place on the premises. Mumford said they couldn't make it stick because other officers had permission to work there."

She slid the paper on the table to me, "On the paper is a list of officers who have had permission to work at the bar. He said the paperwork giving permission to the other officers might get lost, but the officers can be subpoenaed if necessary. Also, the FOP should have records of officers who have had disciplinary action taken for not having permission to work off duty. Apparently, some have had suspensions, but none have been fired. He did say if the police found out there was a leak, his source would be ferreted out and fired. Mumford doesn't want his source fired. I think John needs to get this information to Mr. Fellows."

Sarah and Dad were looking at me expecting a response. I took a minute to mull over what she had said before answering, "Fellows suspected I might be fired due to political considerations. The election is soon, and the mayor doesn't want any bad publicity. I'll call Fellows in the morning. I agree he should know about this."

"I can understand their ploy," Dad stated. "If the department can get the media to buy into their reasoning, then the public will think they're not responsible for John's actions. In effect, they're washing their hands of the whole matter before the election. They'll fire John, but they're not worried about him getting his job back. In fact, I don't think they care one way or the other."

He continued tapping his right index finger on the table. "You'll file suit to get your job back. They can delay the hearing by using procedural matters long enough for the election to be over before the suit comes to trial. During the campaign, the mayor can say neither he nor the police department sanctioned John's actions. Corrective action was taken as soon as the facts came to light – end of matter."

"Pretty damn slimy," Sarah flared!

"What did you expect? They're politicians," he answered as more of a statement than question.

***

My cell phone rang. The caller ID showed it was Sgt. Hickman. When I answered, Hickman got directly to the point, "John, homicide picked up Treece's buddy – Ali Johnson. Detective Wilson's questioning him, but Johnson's not cooperating. He's already asked for an attorney. We don't have any evidence to hold him. Wilson will have to kick him loose."

Crap, there wasn't even circumstantial evidence to hold him. I couldn't identify him. I only saw his back as he ran away. Everything was hearsay from the streets. I felt hopeless.

"I'm coming by your house when shift ends. We're going to take a ride," Hickman said.

"Where?" I asked.

"I'll tell you when I pick you up," he answered.

***

I could tell neither Dad nor Sarah liked the idea of me going with Hickman without any explanation of where we were going. I didn't argue with either. I just told them I had to trust his judgment. When Hickman arrived at half past midnight, he was dressed in civilian clothes. He was using his personal car. After a quick introduction to my dad, we left.

In the car, he asked, "Are you carrying?"

"I've got my Glock 27," I answered. I was nervous, but my interest peaked.

"Good. I've got a reliable snitch who says Frank's bar girl is working at the Pussy Cat Lounge giving lap dances. Same game… just a different bar. We'll go by and have a chat with her. I want you with me so I know it's her. The CI could have the wrong woman."

I didn't feel good about this remembering the major's question about interfering. I blurted out exactly what flashed into my mind, "Aren't we

77

interfering with an investigation? Obstruction of justice? We both could get in trouble."

"I've got 30 years in," Hickman answered stealing a glance at me. "I'm a dinosaur – a throwback to the old days of policing. Nothing wrong with going to a bar having a drink with a friend. If we learn something, then I'll pass it to Detective Wilson. He'll keep quiet about how he got the information. He's on our side."

"That's really walking a fine line," I answered feeling uneasy.

"That's the problem with the younger cops," he retorted. "You worry too much. Ninety percent of the time, there's nothing you can do about a problem. Concentrate on the ten percent you can do something about."

***

The Pussy Cat Lounge was a dive. It was located in a seedy party of downtown. Bright pink neon letters announced its presence in a deteriorating brick building. The adjacent parking lot had minimum light which I assumed was so the girls could conduct their business without drawing attention to them. Hickman parked on the street a block away from the bar. We sat in the front seat watching as a skimpy dressed woman led a man around the corner to a car. In a short time, we could see the man's head in the car's front seat but not the woman's.

Shaking his head, Hickman stated, "The world's oldest profession is alive and well. Let's go see if we can find her."

A large burly man was guarding the main entrance. He wore faded jeans with a leather biker's jacket over a black tee shirt with a faded symbol of a white fist on the front of the shirt. His hair was closely cropped. On the side of his neck was a tattoo of an iron cross. He gave us a hard look as we passed. A faint odor of marijuana emanated off his clothes. I decided he was a dangerous man and gave him as wide a berth as possible while Hickman seemed oblivious to him. Hickman gave a faint nod to the man as he passed.

The inside was what I can only describe as a dump. It took a moment for my eyes to adjust to the dim lighting. The floor was wood planking. It looked like the finish had been worn off the floor for years. The side walls were lined with booths which had curtains that could be drawn supposedly giving privacy when a "client" was given a lap dance. The booths' seats

78

were dark cranberry colored vinyl. The vinyl showed white cracks from use and age.

A tall bar blocked the back wall so the bartenders could keep an eye on the activity. There were no stools at the bar. It was painted with cheap shiny enamel. The men behind the bar looked more like thugs than bartenders. Their bodies were decorated with an assortment of tattoos. I was too far away to tell what the tattoos were. A fight wouldn't last long here. I seriously doubted if the police would ever be called after the fight.

Old wooden tables crowded the center of the room. Sturdy built wooden chairs were clustered around the tables. The same paint had been used on them. The bar owners hadn't spent much money on decorations. Of course, the patrons weren't in the bar for its ambiance. There weren't many customers. Only one booth was occupied. It had the curtains drawn. I suppose a girl was giving a lap dance or something else.

I was surprised when Hickman took a seat at one of the first tables with his back facing the door. Police officers like to sit with their backs to a wall so they can observe who is coming into the establishment and know what is happening around them. I sat catty-cornered to the sergeant. At least one of us could see the entrance. Hickman whispered, "The dude at the door is a confidential informant. He's been a snitch for some time – a petty criminal. We could bust him anytime we want, and he knows it. He'll tip me off if trouble heads our way.""

Hickman stopped talking as one of the bartenders approached our table. He made no pretense about examining us. Both his forearms were tattooed with Aryan symbols. I could smell whiskey on his breath when he asked, "What're you guys having?"

"Weller on the rocks for both of us," Hickman answered.

The man nodded and walked back to the bar. I watched him pouring the whiskey as he signaled a woman to take the drinks to us. I thought there was something familiar about the woman as she approached. I recognized her when she was ten feet from our table. She was Brandy. She had dyed her hair jet black. Her low cut dress was so short it barely covered her crotch. A generous view of cleavage was enhanced by a push up bra. There was recognition in her eyes as she sat the drinks on the table. Hickman saw it too.

"Can I buy you a drink?" Hickman asked.

"I'm busy waiting tables," she nervously answered.

"I think you can find the time to have a drink with us," snapped Hickman. "Or, you'll find the time to go downtown. It's your choice."

Beads of sweat formed on her brow as she glanced over her should at the bar. It'll cost you twenty dollars. I only drink Champaign cocktails."

Hickman took a roll of bills out of his pocket peeling off two twenties. "Twenty for your drink and twenty for ours."

She picked up the bills walking quickly to the bar. As she handed the money to a bartender, there was a quick exchange of words with her glancing in our direction. The bartender focused his attention on us as she spoke. A Champaign glass, which I was certain contained only ginger ale, was given to her. Hickman's head swiveled around like a radar mast taking in all movement in the bar. The man left the bar and knocked on a door behind it. He disappeared behind the door.

Brandy sauntered towards us. There was an exaggerated sway of the hips. I saw glimpses of her black panties. Brandy took a seat facing me. Her eyes flickered between Hickman and the bar.

Hickman spoke first, asking, "What's your name?"

"Alice," she cooed.

"Your real name! Not Alice, not Brandy... What is your legal name?" growled Hickman.

"What's in a name? Alice, Brandy, I can be any name you want," she answered with drops of perspiration streaking the heavy makeup on her temples.

"Don't play cute with me. I'm not playing games with you," Hickman said angrily as he leaned forward. "Downtown might change your attitude."

Fear came into her face as she whimpered, "My name is Janice. I swear to God!"

A monster sized man came out of the office. He skirted around the bar walking directly towards us. He took a seat two tables from us. His head was shaved clean with Nazi symbols tattooed on the skull. Each of his digits had a letter tattooed spelling out white power. He was the classic Aryan supremacist skinhead. There was a suspicious bulge under his shirt at the right hip – probably a gun. He made no pretense. He sat at the table staring at us.

"I want a last name," Hickman ordered keeping his voice low enough that the skinhead couldn't hear him.

Janice, or whatever her real name was, appeared terrified. She kept her eyes downcast stealing glances at the skinhead as she barely moved her lips, "You've got to leave! I can't talk here! They'll hurt me! I'll meet with you in the next couple of days. I swear! I've just got to figure out how to do it. Give me a way to contact you. I'm begging you! Just leave!"

Fear affects people different ways. I could tell she was losing control. Hickman said, "Call the police department. Ask for Sergeant Hickman."

Hickman didn't leave his card. The chair legs screeched on the floor as he stood. He motioned with his head for me to follow. Hickman didn't speak or look back as we exited onto the sidewalk. Once we were a little distance from the bar, he said, "There's a hell of a lot more going on than Frank getting a little on the side if my instincts are correct. That woman's frightened for her life, and I believe her."

I remained silent thinking. What was really going on? Motive is a big piece of the puzzle when solving a crime. In some crimes the motive is straight forward. In a robbery, the motive is money. The simple explanation would be she was a prostitute, and the skinheads were her pimps. It's common practice for pimps to use violence to control their whores. That could be the answer in a nutshell.

Glancing over my shoulder, I saw the skinhead from the table standing beside Hickman's CI. They were watching us. After we got into Hickman's car, he made a sharp U-turn speeding away from the bar. We were parked far enough away that they couldn't read the license plate numbers, and the speed limited the time they could see the car. Using the internet, it is not difficult to trace plates if you're willing to spend a few bucks. We drove a few minutes in silence before Hickman asked, "John, what's your take on the situation?"

"She knows something but is scared to talk. Those skinheads are running a prostitution ring. It must make them a lot of money," I answered.

"That's obvious," Hickman said thoughtfully. "But, how did Frank Glass fit into the equation? Why would somebody want to kill Glass? They wouldn't kill him just because he was hitting on one of the prostitutes. It'd bring too much heat."

***

Everybody was asleep when I got home. I slipped into our bedroom trying to be quiet, but I felt filthy. I had already bathed that evening but being in the bar left me feeling dirty. I thought it was probably subconscious. I went into the bathroom shutting the door to keep the light from disturbing Sarah.

After stripping off my clothes, I got the shower as hot as I thought I could stand. When I got into the shower, I thought I was going to pass out. The wounds from the glass shards shot waves of pain through my body. It was everything I could do to keep from screaming. I let the water cascade over my body until my skin was bright pink. I still felt soiled when I got out.

Sarah mumbled a few uninterpretable words and went back to sleep. My night was restless. My mind kept trying to make a logical connection between Frank, the skinheads, Janice and Dejuan Treece. It didn't make sense. An Aryan supremacist group wouldn't deal with a black gang, and the reverse was true. It'd be like making a pact with the devil for both groups. The woman and skinheads made sense. She was a source of revenue – property of the skinheads. Where did Frank fit into the picture? The most logical conclusion would be he didn't. We were in the wrong place at the wrong time. We were hired to give the bar an appearance of legitimacy.

CHAPTER 9

The smell of coffee and squeals of laughter from Amy woke me in the morning. Sarah had slipped out of bed without waking me. When I entered the kitchen, Dad was on the floor playing with Amy. Apparently he had done no better feeding her than I had because she had food smeared over her face. Smiling, Dad looked up at me, "Sarah's left for work. She said her arm's really sore. I think I've fed Amy, but I'm not too sure. She may have more food on her than in her."

"The apple doesn't fall far from the tree," I joked. "That's the way she looks when I feed her. I'll give her a bath. Think Mom would be willing to watch her for a while? I'd like to get the posts set for the deck."

"You don't have to ask," he laughed. "I'll take Amy to her after you get her clean."

After Dad left with Amy, I called Fellows' office and brought him up to date on Sarah's meeting with the reporter Mumford. Fellows gave the impression he wasn't surprised about the plans for terminating me. His assessment of the situation was close to Dad's opinion. His last statement before ending the call was, "Some political animals have no compunction about morals. Their whole purpose in life is about winning. The companion of winning is power, and power is the nectar of those politicians."

As soon as I hung up the phone, the doorbell rang. Because I didn't expect any visitors, I got my pistol holding it behind my back. I cracked the door being careful to stand behind the wall, allowing the door to give me a minimum of cover. After everything that had happened, I wasn't going to take any chances. Detective Wilson was getting ready knock on the door. Wilson stood on the porch not asking to enter, "Sergeant Hickman filled me in on your road trip last night. The woman you saw is in the hospital in critical condition."

"What happened?" I asked as I slid the pistol into the back of my pants. "How do you know the woman in the hospital is the same woman we saw last night?"

"A call came in this morning from the hospital to Hickman. A woman was found dumped in the park on 23rd Street. There was no ID on the woman. She wouldn't give the hospital her name or any information. She's registered as a Jane Doe. She was severely beaten and asked for the hospital staff to call Hickman at the police department," Wilson answered ignoring my tucking the pistol in my pants.

"Hickman went to the hospital. He confirmed it was her. She asked him to speak to you specifically. She wouldn't answer any of Hickman's questions. She said she'd only talk to you. Hickman said she was in bad shape. The doctors said she had a brain bleed with swelling and might not make it if they can't get the swelling under control."

"You want me to go talk to her?" I asked.

"No, I want us to go talk to her," Wilson answered sharply!

I told Wilson to come into the house while I scribbled a note to my dad telling him I'd be gone a couple of hours and would explain when I got back. I quickly changed into dress slacks. I put the Glock in a holster. The holster went inside my pants at the hip. I wore a pull over shirt concealing the pistol. After slipping on a pair of low cut shoes, I followed Wilson to his car. Backing out of my drive way, the detective said, "I wish the hell you guys had called me before you went out on your own. We might have avoided the woman getting hurt."

"The last thing on my mind was getting her hurt," I responded. "I'm sure the sarge didn't want her hurt. She was upset and asked us to leave. She said that she'd contact him later. We left because of how scared she was. Apparently, she had cause to be frightened."

"I know," he said glancing at me. "Hickman covered that with me. You guys were walking on thin ice going there. I understand what the sarge was trying to do, but if I had been with you, I could have taken her into protective custody or charged her with something to get her out of there. We could have avoided this mess. We might have gotten some useful information."

"I'm already up to my ass in alligators. What'll happen to the sarge? How much trouble is he in?" I asked.

"It's according to how you want to look at it," he answered. "Technically, it could be construed he was interfering with an ongoing investigation – obstruction. However, it could be argued he was having a drink socially with you and happened to run into her."

"How are you going to report it?" I asked probing to see where he stood.

Wilson didn't immediately answer my question. I could tell he was deciding whether to answer or not. After a few seconds, he said, "I'm going to write it up as a coincidental contact. If she gives us nothing pertaining to the case and providing she doesn't die, I'll turn it over to somebody. My plate's pretty full."

We rode in silence to the University Hospital trauma center. Each man was absorbed in his own thoughts. What did she want to tell me? Was it about her relationship with Frank? Was Frank involved in some kind of criminal activity? Money's a lure that snares some police officers. If the officer is caught, it taints the whole profession in the eyes of the public. I decided to stop making up scenarios. I'd know soon enough.

The hospital was a mammoth concrete structure representing the architecture of the sixties. Wilson drove to the back of the building to the entrance of the emergency room parking in a slot reserved for police. All shootings, knifings and major trauma were brought to University Hospital. The exterior concrete walls by the emergency room entrance were stained from oil from countless hands of people leaning against them waiting their turn to enter. The hospital serviced the poor of the community who couldn't afford care. It was usually crammed to capacity plus a few.

Wilson flashed his badge allowing us to bypass security. The guard at the front desk pressed a button opening a set of large metal doors into the main treatment area of the ER. Apparently Wilson knew his way around the ER. He went directly to the doctor's station showing his badge to one of the interns dressed in pale green scrubs sitting at a computer terminal. The boyish looking doctor immediately stood asking if he could help us. Wilson explained what we wanted. The intern came around the station's waist high wall motioning for us to follow.

The ER's noise assaulted my ears with electron beeping of monitors, pumps and moaning. I wondered how the medical personnel could think with the distracting sounds. Then I thought about our police radios. There is constant communication on the radio. Officers learn to tune out the calls that don't concern them. I assumed medical personnel hear the important sounds while ignoring the ambient noise.

The doctor stopped in front of a beige concrete block room with large sliding glass panels. He pointed at the patient inside the room saying, "We haven't been able to stop the brain bleed or swelling. She's been intubated and sedated."

"Will she make it?" Wilson asked.

"I don't know. Only time will tell," answered the doctor.

The intern slid one of the panels open, and we followed him into the room. To me, it was like entering a macabre chamber. A large clear plastic tube from the woman's mouth was connected to a machine which hissed every few seconds. When the machine hissed, the woman's chest would rise. A smaller tube with greenish material ran from her nose to a suction device on the wall. Several pumps were on a stainless steel pole pumping fluids into the multiple IV's in her arms. One machine pumped a clear liquid while a second machine pumped milk colored fluid into her body. Her face was mauled.

"She has multiple contusions, facial fractures, and six fractured ribs," the intern stated as if reading from a textbook. "From the multiple points of bruising, it appears she was struck with a fist on the facial area."

He lowered her sheet exposing the upper torso before continuing, "Note the crisscross pattern of bruising across the chest. The same pattern is on her back. I'd venture she was whipped with a belt. We intubated her after the loss of consciousness from respiratory difficulties. The increase in intracranial pressure due to the bruising of the brain and the bleeding is due to repeated blows to the head."

Pulling the sheet up to cover her, the doctor added, "Somebody beat the hell out of her. I hope you catch him."

"I appreciate your time," Wilson told the doctor handing him a business card. "If there's any change, one way or the other, please give me a call."

On the drive back to my house, I could tell Wilson was angry. I couldn't discern whether he was angry with Hickman and me or at the animal who had beaten the woman. Perhaps, he was angry at all parties involved. Finally he spoke, "There's no way Hickman or you would have suspected something like this would happen. It's those fucking skinheads. They're paranoid. They tortured her to find out if she talked. When they were finished, they dumped her in the park to die."

"Stay away from that bar!" he ordered. "When I get back to the office, I'll see what the gang unit has on those guys. I think it's time to pay them a visit."

***

When we got home, I saw Dad's pickup truck in the driveway. Wilson dropped me off saying he was going directly to the office. Walking up the driveway, I heard hammering from the backyard. I decided to tell Dad I was home before changing into work clothes. I turned the corner and saw Dad with a sledge hammer pounding a post. He had dug a hole for concrete. He was anchoring the post in the hole by driving it a few inches into the earth to keep it straight. I remained silent until he finished, not that he could have heard me over the loud blows from the sledgehammer.

When he was satisfied the post was secure, he laid the sledgehammer on the ground. Dad made his living using tools. They were too valuable to him to take a chance of damaging them by carelessness. He often told me a project could be done in half the time with better results with the proper tools. A perfect rectangle had been staked in white twine where the deck would be. As usual, Dad had a detailed plan before starting a project.

It was what I would call an "ah ha" moment. I haven't had a plan or used any of the tools available to me since the beginning of this disaster. Craftsmen gather material and use their tools to build. Police officers gather evidence by using their investigative tools to build cases. In both instances, a blueprint is needed to stay on track. I hadn't formulated a plan on how to use the information that I had to defend myself.

When Dad noticed me, I said, "Let's go have a cup of coffee, and I'll fill you in."

By the time I changed clothes, Dad had two cups of coffee on the table. I sat facing him bringing him up to date. He sipped his coffee never interrupting. His focus was intense. He waited for me to finish before asking, "John, do you want my input?"

"Yes, it would be helpful," I answered.

"Correct me if I'm wrong," my father said. "You're still considered an officer although your police powers are suspended. Officially, you can't investigate what's happened. As I said before, I believe the political powers aren't interested in the truth. They're more interested in getting it out of the news. They'll use more man hours building a case against you than in divining what really happened."

"I'm afraid that's probably the truth," I answered.

"Let's put down everything that's happened on paper," he said. "Perhaps we can make some sense out of this."

We ended up using a piece of poster board Sarah had in our closet. Dad drew squares writing a different incident in each square using a timeline. We discussed each incident before placing the incidents in squares that ended up resembling a fishbone. Written in the top square was the "Double H Lounge". There were five separate squares underneath it containing the following information: "Brandy, Frank Glass, Dejuan Treece, Ali Johnson and me". Then there was only one square. It had "drive by shooting". The next line had four squares: "Pussy Cat Lounge, Brandy, confidential informant, and skinheads". The final square had "hospital". It was a rough timeline.

We started drawing double headed arrows between squares we felt had some kind of connection. When we were finished, all the squares had connections. Dejuan Treece and Ali Johnson were only connected to the bar. Dad scratched his jaw staring at the chart, "Let's connect the gang bangers with the drive by shooting – that's logical. I wonder if there's a connection between them and the skinheads."

"I don't think so," I commented. "They hate each other."

Dad drew a dotted line from Treece and Johnson to the skinheads before saying, "Never assume anything. If you do, you can make an ass out of you and me. Why don't you call Sergeant Hickman? Have him take a look at this. Maybe he'll have some ideas."

***

Hickman agreed to come by the house. I was surprised to see Detective Wilson with him when he arrived. Hickman, Wilson and I sat at the table while Dad got coffee for everyone. Hickman and Wilson were studying our chart exchanging glances at each other. Wilson was the first to speak, "Everything spoken here stays confidential. Understood? I'm putting my ass on the line being here!"

Each man nodded before Wilson continued, "John, I've got some really bad news. I hear they're going to fire you. The chief wants to take your case to the grand jury. He wants an indictment for manslaughter. The forensics shows Glass being shot from behind. The exit wound was out the front of the leg. They think they have enough evidence to convict. I think they're looking for you to plea bargain the charge down with probation. That way, you couldn't protest being terminated."

I was stunned. Not only were they going to fire me, but they were going to prosecute. I did not shoot Frank! My thoughts were interrupted when Hickman angrily said, "They don't have enough evidence to convict John. The bastards are throwing John under the bus for political expediency! They could give a crap about what really happened."

"I believe that is the case; otherwise, I wouldn't be here. It's up to us to solve this case. Now, let's get down to business," Wilson answered. "I had an interesting discussion with the gang unit this morning. The skinheads are running a sophisticated organization that's attracted the attention of the FBI and BTAF. They have straw corporations running three bars in our area. They're involved in prostitution, drugs and gun running. Their enforcers are ruthless. Their women are considered property. They have a compound in a neighboring county which is rumored to be fortified with heavy machine guns and even mines. Neither federal organization has been able to infiltrate them."

"Any information on how they get their drugs or distribute them?" asked Hickman.

"Nothing that can be tied to them," answered Wilson.

"I have a CI in the skinheads," Hickman informed the detective holding his palms upward as if apologizing. "Obviously, he's been holding back on me."

Wilson looked pissed as he sarcastically replied, "It'd been nice if you'd told me. Never the less, we may be able to use your CI. Put a lot of pressure on him. I don't think he'll talk. He knows they'll kill him if they find out."

"Where's their compound," Dad asked interrupting the exchange.

"Why do you want to know?" asked Wilson with an implication that it was none of Dad's business.

Dad appeared not to have taken offense, "You need information. I may be able to help. I never speak about what I did in Vietnam. I've tried to put it out of my mind. I was a sniper in Vietnam. Some of my assignments were and probably still are classified. Yes, I did terminate some individuals which is the politically correct way of saying I killed some people. My primary mission was to gather Intel on many of my assignments. Snipers are trained to observe and not be seen."

Wilson glared at the older man rapping his fingers on the table before asking, "How are you going to get information?"

"I can slip up to their headquarters undetected," Dad answered locking eyes with the detective. "They'll never know they're being watched. No organization can work in isolation. With a little luck, I can get pictures of the people associating with the skinheads. They have to be doing business with outsiders. I'll give the pictures to you. It might fill in some of the missing pieces in this puzzle if you can identify the players."

Reluctantly Wilson gave Dad the address of the skinhead's compound. He swore he'd disavow knowing anything if Dad got into trouble. It didn't help ease the tension between the two of them when Dad quipped, "Been there, done that."

***

After Hickman and Wilson had left, Dad asked me to go with him to his house. Mom had left a note on the kitchen table saying she had taken Amy to the park. I followed him into a room he had converted into an office. I was surprised at all the equipment. On an L shaped desk in the corner sat an oversized LCD monitor, a high quality printer and a tower computer under the desk. Dad took a folding chair out of the closet placing it next to an executive rolling chair. He motioned for me to sit in the folding chair as he sat and fired up the computer.

He had a devilish grin before saying, "Bet you didn't think your old man knew anything about computers. I had too much time on my hands when I retired. I took a couple of courses in using personal computers. I like messing around with them. I found that there's a lot of free information on the internet. Some of it is sound. Some of it is garbage."

He clicked on the Google Earth icon typing in our state for a search. Zeroing in on the area he wanted, he shifted the screen centering the skinhead's compound before speaking, "Some of these guys must be ex military by their choice of location and how it's laid out."

Their entrance was off a winding two lane blacktopped county road in the middle of nowhere. The driveway was a single gravel road that I'd estimate was a mile long leading to a ten acre field which was surrounded by several hundred acres of forest. In the middle of the field were several small buildings clustered around a larger building. Two parallel fences were on the perimeter."

"I'd say it's most unusual for civilians to have this tight of security," Dad stated studying the screen. "It looks like they're prepared for a siege. There's a small water tower and a large generator behind the large building. I'd bet there are propane tanks buried to supply the generator. Satellite dishes on the roof for communication. Why not just wave a red flag telling the Feds to look at me?"

"There's nothing illegal about their setup," I commented. "You have to have probable cause to get a search warrant even if you suspect it's not kosher. They hide behind the same constitution that they claim to detest."

"The bastards are hiding something," he growled tapping the screen with his forefinger. "I'd bet my ass that building is a kennel. They're using dogs to patrol – probably at night. Those have to be cameras on the poles close to the buildings. I'd say the cameras have infra red capability. The cameras are only as good as the people watching them. The trouble is people get bored watching nothing happen. They tend to be easily distracted ignoring the monitors. I wonder if they have some kind of detectors on the fence. We're going to have to be careful."

Surprise was the least way I could describe the shock I felt when he said "we". It must have shown on my face because Dad winked at me, "Snipers don't work solo. We work in teams. Two sets of eyes and ears are better than one. Of course, you don't have to go if you feel uncomfortable."

An innumerable amount of thoughts flooded into my mind. Technically, what we were contemplating was not illegal unless the area was posted. Regardless, whether it was posted or not, it would be dangerous. Dad felt he needed backup, or he wouldn't have asked me. He was willing to put it all on the line. He had chosen to be part of the battle to clear me which made it a team effort."

"Wouldn't think of letting you go it alone," I answered grasping his shoulder.

CHAPTER 10

Dad decided we had some serious shopping to do. The first stop was at a small sporting goods store. Upon entering and looking at the inventory, I decided it was more of a survivalist shop. It was crammed with MREs, military surplus and other gear. He got two ghillie ponchos instead of suits. He said the ponchos were sufficient for what we were doing, and they were easier and quicker to put on and take off. A camo bag, face paint and rifle wrap completed his purchases. I mentally questioned why he bought the rifle wrap but didn't ask.

The next stop was at a camera store. After listening to a long winded pitch from a salesperson, he bought a digital Nikon camera with a telescopic lens. We spent the next half hour learning the operation of the camera. Satisfied we could operate the camera effectively, he took the camera to the truck putting it in the camo bag. On the drive back, he asked, "I saw a question on you face when I got the rifle wrap. Wondering why?"

"It was that obvious?" I asked. "I suspect you're not going unarmed. I don't know if that's wise."

"Don't plan on using it," he bluntly stated. "One of my rules is never go to a gun fight with empty hands. John, these people are going to be armed to the teeth. I plan on us slipping in and out without them noticing. But, I'm not going to look down the business end of a gun without being able to defend myself."

Now that everything was out in the open, I asked, "What are you taking?"

"A rifle that I'm very familiar with," he answered. "I've got a Winchester model 70 with a Unertl scope. It's chambered for a .308 caliber. I used it in Nam. Anything within a thousand yards is mine. Let's get changed into some work clothes with boots and go take a look at the place. Who knows, we might get lucky."

***

Dad drove the pickup truck about a mile pass the skinhead's compound entrance pulling onto the road's shoulder. He placed a note, which he had written at home, under the wiper blades saying the truck had broken down, he'd be back to get it. He had mapped out a route to the compound bringing us to the rear of it. He wanted to be at the rear for two reasons: to avoid traffic entering or exiting the compound and because most activity usually took place at the rear of living quarters. I couldn't argue with his reasoning.

The area was sparsely populated. We hadn't seen another vehicle in half an hour. I took the camo bag tucking the ghillie poncho under my arm. Dad had his ghillie poncho and the wrapped rifle. We faded into the woods across the road from the truck. Dad led the way to a small creek which the Google picture showed winding close to the rear of the compound. Reaching the creek's bank, Dad held up his hand to stop. It had been agreed there would be no talking once we were in the field.

He used his thumb to smear dark green stripes of paint on the high shiny ridges of my face. Then he did the same to himself. He looked like a character out of a war movie when he was finished. Next he unrolled the ghillie poncho and draped it over his head and shoulders with it hanging down his back. I mimicked him. Satisfied, he motioned for me to follow as he headed into the shallow creek. Hunched over with the poncho covering most of his body, he slowly stepped from stone to stone stopping every few moments to observe and listen.

What would have taken a half hour at a brisk pace, took us over two hours. If it hadn't been early fall, we would have been caught by the dark. I don't think darkness would have bothered Dad in the woods – just me. I lost all sense of location, but Dad was in his element. He motioned for us to stop and pointed to his left indicating that was the direction we were heading. Again using his hand, he signaled he wanted us both lower to the ground. We crept out of the streambed hunched over. Dad looked like a slow moving bush.

We had moved five hundred yards from the creek when he signaled to stop. Without looking at me, he went to the ground in a sloth like motion starting what a sniper would call a high crawl. I tried to imitate his motions, but I wasn't as skilled. Damn, he didn't make any sound as he moved while I could hear the distinct sound of small twigs snapping as I crawled behind him. It was as if he were a ghost.

As we approached the tree line of the compound, Dad switched to a low crawl using his fingers to pull him while pushing with his toes. To me, it took forever to reach the edge of the field. With an all so slow motion of his hand, Dad signaled for me to move next to him. He was looking through his scope by the time I was next to him. In a whisper that I almost couldn't hear, he said, "Get the camera. I think you'll see something very interesting."

The camera had been wrapped in camouflage netting with the metal parts covered with dull green tape. Following Dad's lead, I moved ever so slowly. Once I had the telescopic lens focused on the rear of the compound, I did have a surprise. There were two black men with five skinheads drinking beer from bottles. The gangbangers were flying their colors – red bandanas around their necks. The group was laughing about something, apparently at ease with each other. The skinheads were dressed in black military fatigues while the gangbangers were dressed in what I considered hood clothes.

Crap, talk about a paradigm shift! This whole scene didn't make sense. I pushed those thoughts out of my mind and focused on the mission, as Dad would have called it. I started snapping pictures of their faces. I could see Dad tense when the camera made small buzzing sounds each time I took a picture. Luckily, there was a small breeze blowing towards us which carried the sound away from the compound into the woods.

The atmosphere of the group suddenly shifted from a party mode to a business mode. One of the gangbangers pulled out a thick wad of money from his pants pocket. I kept the camera humming as the transaction took place. The thin man who had sharp features handed the money to a large bald skinhead who had a thick bull neck. The gangbangers didn't seem happy that he counted it. I took it as a sign that there wasn't complete trust between the two groups. The skinhead flashed a wide grin at his group revealing a mouth full of tobacco stained teeth. He nodded for the others to follow him. The group disappeared to the front of the compound.

Dad turned his head and winked at me. He scooted backwards motioning me to follow. As soon as we were deep within the woods, he used a much quicker pace than he had used when he had ingressed. When we reached the creek, Dad took off his ghillie poncho rolling it neatly for carrying. He took a handkerchief from his back pocket wiping off his face paint. Handing the handkerchief to me, he said, "An enemy of my enemy is…"

"A friend," I answered.

"No, a business partner," he corrected.

***

During the drive home, we had a lively discussion. Actually, it was pretty much a one sided discussion with me talking and Dad listening. I ached in places that I didn't know I had. Dad acted like he had a stroll in the park. The black wall of night was rising over the city as we pulled into his driveway. Dad stashed the rifle and ghillie ponchos behind the seat of the truck only taking the camera into his house. We went to his office where he downloaded the pictures to his computer. I had to admit that he was pretty technically savvy.

He used a program to enhance and isolate a color facial of each man printing out an eight by ten photo. He printed several group pictures of the meeting. Finally, he printed a color plus a black and white photo of the exchange of money. He explained that sometimes a black and white photo gave better definition to the human eye explaining it was hard to camouflage anything from a color blind person. They see shades which makes movement and outlines of objects easily identified. He manipulated the program zeroing on the folded bills being exchanged.

I could make out the denomination of the top bill. It was a hundred dollar bill. I estimated the thickness of the stack of bills by the man's thumb holding them. If I was anywhere close, then some serious money was involved. No chump change here. Now the question, what were the gangbangers getting? I suspected, whatever it was, they had gone to the front to get it. Dad had pointed out the suspicious bulges under the gang member's jackets. The skinheads didn't try to conceal their weapons. They wore their pistols openly on their hips. Both sides were carrying enough heat to keep the other side honest.

There was something familiar about the gangbanger who had handled the money. Studying the picture of him, I knew I had seen him before, but where? Stacking all the pictures, I left his on top of the pile. I would place where I had seen him later. It happened to me frequently. The answer would just pop into my mind. I called Detective Wilson asking him to meet us at my house.

***

When Dad and I arrived, Wilson's unmarked unit was parked out front on the street. Entering, I saw Wilson playing with Amy on the floor. They were rolling a ball back and forth. Amy didn't have quite the technique of getting the ball to Wilson, but she was giggling with delight with her new found playmate. Wilson looked up at me smiling, "I've got a rug rat of my own. Don't get to spend enough time with him though. I'm considering taking the sergeant examine and go back into uniform. I'd have a schedule and could spend more time with my family, but I'd miss the overtime pay."

Sarah was getting bowls of food from the oven and said, "Money's not everything, Ken."

"My wife says the same thing," he answered.

I noticed Sarah set four plates on the table. Apparently Wilson was eating with us. Dad and I washed at the kitchen sink before joining Sarah and Wilson at the table. Amy was in her highchair between Sarah and me. Sarah asked for us to join hands before praying, "Lord, we ask not a simple deed. We ask for deliverance of justice. Give us guidance to end the evil that has invaded our lives."

Wilson had bowed his head with closed eyes. He silently mouthed his own prayer as Sarah prayed. I wondered what his prayer was. We didn't discuss what we had found during the meal. The conversation centered on our families. I learned that Wilson's dreams and desires weren't all that different from mine.

We all worked together clearing the table and washing dishes with Wilson in the middle of the activity. Everything had been cleaned and put away before we sat down at the table again. It struck me that most of the

97

time people ended up in the kitchen when socially interacting. I believe sharing food is a bonding experience dating back to prehistoric times when food was scarce and offering a share was truly giving of oneself.

Dad laid the stack of photos in the center of the table. Wilson immediately picked up the top photograph furrowing his brow moving his jaw like he was grinding his teeth. "Do you know who this is?" he asked me.

"He looks familiar, but I can't place him," I answered.

"It's Ali Johnson – the other gang member at the shooting," he stated.

Memories flooded my mind. I had only caught a glimpse of the fleeing second man. The angular features! That's what I remember! Things happened too fast, and it was too damn dark for me to make a definite ID. What was he doing with the skinheads? Wilson interrupted my thoughts, "This puts a different twist on the matter."

"Now we know the Perros have some kind of arrangement with the skinheads," he continued raising a forefinger for emphasis. "Treece and Johnson were walking towards the Double H Lounge which we know is a skinhead operation. Were they making a drop? Or, were they doing a pickup? The only common denominator that I can see is drugs. Now the question is who is supplying whom?"

"This may answer your question," Dad said thumbing through the photos removing the ones showing the exchange of money.

Wilson took the pictures giving out a low whistle, "Hundred dollar bills. Must be at least five grand there, maybe ten. Looks like the skinheads are bringing in the drugs, and the Perros are distributing them. It's a pact between devils. I'll share this information with narcotics and DEA. If we can catch the Perros with a shipment, I'm sure they'll deal and drop the skinheads in the bucket. No loyalty between those two groups."

"Did you get any pictures of the product exchange?" Wilson asked.

"No," Dad answered. "We were at the rear of the compound. They went to the front after the money was exchanged. I'd bet their vehicle was parked in the front. We couldn't see what they put in their vehicle, or what type of vehicle they were using."

"It's a shame. It might have given us an idea of what kind of drug they're selling. Ten grand of marijuana would be bulky while cocaine would be smaller in volume. Nice job on gathering intel, but I'd recommend staying away. I'm sure the DEA will have observers at the compound after I give them this information."

"I'll take your advice under consideration," answered Dad with a thin smile.

After Wilson had left, Sarah, Dad and I discussed the meeting. Dad didn't have much to say and left. Sarah put Amy in her crib while I took a shower. I absent mindedly watched the water circle the drain cleansing the evidence of my day's activity. What we had gathered was good information, but I couldn't see how it would help clear me. I was a victim of being in the wrong place at the wrong time."

***

I was in the back yard hosing out the wheelbarrow. I had just finished pouring cement around the deck posts. Sarah had taken Amy to my mom before going to work. Dad had called to say he had some errands. All morning I couldn't get the shooting out of my mind. I think the shrinks would classify it as obsessive compulsive behavior. It was easy for them to put me in a category. They didn't have my problem without a foreseeable solution.

I had left the back door open letting in fresh air through the screened door. I heard the doorbell ring. I walked around the side of the house rather than go through it. Glancing at my watch, I noticed it was 1:00 P.M. I had worked through lunch and realized my stomach was growling. Turning the front corner, I saw our postal carrier standing on the front porch with a letter in his hand. With minimum speech, he had me sign for a certified letter.

I just stared at the envelope as I returned to the backyard. It was from the police department. I sat on the back steps holding my breath as I ripped it open. It was from the personnel department. The letter stated I was terminated effective yesterday for breaking departmental policy. I had the right to appeal the termination contractually. Arrangement would be made for turning in all departmental equipment.

No matter how much you think you're prepared for something like this, it's a big blow to the psyche. I shut down mentally just looking at the smudge prints on the paper from my hands. It's amazing how the brain can shut down when it's overloaded with pain whether it's physical or it's psychological. The ringing of the phone inside the house snapped me out of my trance. I refolded the letter and slipped it back into the envelope as I walked into the house.

It was Henry Fellows on the line, "This Henry Fellows. May I speak to John Drake?"

"Mr. Fellows," I blurted out. "I've been fired!"

"I know," he answered. "I've been in court this morning. When I got back to the office, I had a copy of the letter on my desk being I'm representing you. Also, I was informed that they're taking your case to the grand jury for an indictment pertaining to the death of Officer Frank Glass. I suspect the charge will be either manslaughter or reckless homicide."

I thought I was going to pass out. I became light headed, and my knees started to buckle as I stumbled to a nearby chair. Fellows must have heard my panicked breathing because he asked, "John, are you OK?"

"Give me a second," I answered laying the phone in my lap rubbing my face with both hands. I took several slow deep breaths trying to regain enough composure to rationally listen to Fellows. My voice sounded abnormally high as I said, "I expected to be fired, but the indictment was a shock!"

"I'm rather surprised myself that they moved so quickly," answered Fellows. "Remember, an indictment is the possibility of bringing charges against you. If the grand jury delivers a true bill, then you'll be charged. If they believe there's not enough evidence to convict, then there will be no charge. We are not given the opportunity to present our side of the case to the grand jury. It's a one sided presentation, and its findings are held secret. John, there are a lot of if's. If you are charged, then it will go to a jury trial. They'll have to show us all evidence before going to trial – no surprises. Personally, I think they don't believe they have enough to convict. It's political grandstanding to appease."

"Appease who?" I asked.

"Certain segments of society and the press," he answered. "There's nothing you can do at this time. Stay away from the press and let me handle it."

I informed Fellows about yesterday. After I had finished, he said, "It might explain why Johnson and Treece were there, but it doesn't identify who shot the officer. I think they'll choose to ignore the information claiming it has no direct bearing on who pulled the trigger although I feel otherwise."

Thoughts that Sarah would call "demons" invaded my mind after talking to Fellows. Sarah said demons thrived on fear. The more fear, the bigger the portal for them to enter and play with your mind. Immediately I thought about going to prison. Convicted cops don't do well in prison – if they manage to survive. Routinely, for their own protection, they're isolated from the prison's general population because it's too easy to have a shank shoved between the ribs. Isolation, within itself, can be a hell. Without outside communication, people have been known to go insane. Would I be one of them?

I took the phone quickly dialing Sarah's office knowing she could help drive the demons away. Sarah answered and words spilled out of me, "It's worse than I ever thought it could be! They not only fired me, but they're indicting me!"

"Bastards!" she growled. "What's the indictment?"

"For the death of the other officer," I answered with my voice starting to crack. "Fellows said they'd indict me for manslaughter or reckless homicide."

Sarah was quiet for a few seconds before responding, "They might be able to convince the grand jury to bring charges, but I don't think they'll be able to win. John, they're going to drag you through the mud, but you have to stay strong. Do you want me to come home?"

"No," I answered although I really would have liked her to be with me. "I need to settle down and get my head back on straight."

I pushed the end button placing the phone back in its holder. I opened a cabinet reaching for a bottle of whiskey. For an unexplainable reason, I rested my hand on the bottle without picking it up. No, alcohol wasn't the solution to my problem. It may temporarily numb my mind, but the problem wasn't going away. I'd be swapping one problem for another.

Slowly closing the cabinet door, I decided to finish putting away my tools. Perhaps, working with my hands would push the thoughts from my mind. Perhaps, putting my tools in order would mimic putting my life back in order. Perhaps, there was wisdom in Dad's philosophy about life. I thought about several of his axioms: worry about only the things you can do something about because ninety percent of the things that happen in life you cannot do anything about, nobody said life was fair and pick your time and place for battle.

I went outside putting my hand tools in the wheelbarrow and taking it to the garage. I decided to clean the garage. I'd put all my tools in order. I actually smiled. I was taking a symbolic step towards putting my life in order. Dad was in construction. He built tangible things that you could see and put your hands on. I was a cop. I built intangible things such as cases. You couldn't put your hands on a case, but it was just as important to society. I realized we were alike in many ways.

I heard two short taps from a car horn. Walking out of the garage, I saw Dad ambling towards me. He looked tired. I could see dark areas under his eyes. He was shaking his head as he said, "Pinhead and his puppet were on the radio."

I knew who he was speaking about. Pinhead was the mayor. Citizens who were less than enthralled about his administration had nicknamed him pinhead because his head appeared to be much too small for his bloated body. Even the newspaper editorial cartoons emphasized the discrepancy. His contempt for the police was thinly veiled. It was widely rumored that his sexual taste was what the general public would consider out of the norm. I had no firsthand knowledge. I shied away from the discussions in the locker room.

The Chief of Police, an appointed position, carried out the mayor's policies without question. The mayor said there were no gangs in the city; therefore, the gang unit was dissolved. In its place, a Special Roaming Unit or SRU was created. The SRU was supposed to concentrate on hot spots of criminal activity in the city until it was suppressed. Then, the unit would move to the next blaze.

The chief pointed out to the media that it saved the city money and gave flexibility to the department. In actuality, it cost the city additional funds because of the overtime and took pressure off the gangs. The gang unit knew the active players. The SRU lost contact with the gangs because of constantly moving. The gang unit had to be re-implemented.

"I guess you know?" I asked.

"Yep, its bullshit!" he answered angrily. "Hope that son of a bitch gets caught with one of his little boyfriends! That'd cost him the election!"

Dad gave a gyrating motion with his hips eliciting a laugh from both of us. It hit me like a ton of bricks. Damn, Dad was human after all with a sense of humor. I remembered Mark Twain's quote, "When I was a boy of 14, my father was so ignorant I could hardly stand to have the old man around. But when I got to be 21, I was astonished at how much he had learned in seven years."

With that quote in mind, I asked, "How do you think this mess will end up?"

Dad became quiet locking eyes with me, "I don't know, but as Shakespeare said in Henry the Fifth, "Once more unto the breach, dear friends, once more." John, you can't back down. They'll keep attacking you and trying to wear you down. I'm positive that there'll be offers made. Screw 'em. You did nothing wrong. You don't have to accept any offer other than to clear your name. Soldiers die in battle from friendly fire. I'm not saying you shot the other officer. I don't believe that. What I'm trying to get across is that I believe you and support you. This is a battle, and I'll follow you unto the breach."

Tears formed in my eyes as I went to my father and hugged him. We stood hugging each other, both men silently weeping on the inside.

CHAPTER 11

Sarah arrived home toting Amy on her hip. I was at the stove trying to prepare supper with emphasis on "trying". I'm not much of a cook, but I *can* open cans of vegetables. I had some crumbled hamburger in the skillet with plans of making a white sauce. It'd be a sort of creamed beef layered on toast. Well, that was my plan. Like all great plans, it was going to hell. I had flour scattered over the top of the stove with a random assortment of pots coming to boil.

Sarah, being a goddess of wisdom, surveyed the situation and handed me Amy gently nudging us out of the way as she put on an apron. With her back to me, trying to make some order out of my well thought out plan, she said, "Mark Mumford called me today. He said city hall is leaking like a sieve. His source said the district attorney's case hinges entirely on the forensic report that the other officer was shot from the rear. Nothing new there. Only two shell casings were found. There were 13 rounds in your magazine. The man you shot had two gunshot wounds."

"That should prove I didn't shoot Frank," I said.

"John, it's not that simple," she answered. "Mumford said they're going to imply that you had an extra round in the chamber for a total of 16 rounds. They have some officers who will give testimony that it's common practice for some officers although it's against policy. They'll point out that no witness has come forward saying they saw another gunman or heard a shot from behind you."

"Guilty from lack of evidence," I said.

"No," she answered. "The DA believes he can convince the grand jury to bring a true bill, but he has reservations about a conviction. The mayor pushed him to indict. Mumford said the DA will probably hand the case off to one of his assistant prosecutors. The DA can blame his assistant for losing the case. He has a dismal track record against Henry Fellows – hasn't won a case against him.

"It has nothing to do with whether you're innocent or not. By the time discovery and the legal wrangling take place, the election will be over. They figure they'll be re-elected. You'll be old news. They'll play it off as they did the right thing – win or lose. It won't matter to them."

Sarah managed to salvage the meal. It was quite good. Having missed lunch, I over ate. I rationalized it as compensating for lunch. I could afford to put on a few pounds. I had lost a lot of weight when we were separated. My clothes were a couple of sizes too large now. Loneliness is not a good diet. I know.

Supper was finished, and we fell into our normal routine. I bathed Amy, who loved the white sauce but managed to deposit the vegetables in her hair and on her clothes, while Sarah cleared the table. With only four inches of warm water in the bathtub, Amy was in paradise. Through experience, I was prepared. I had a bath towel draped around my neck and over my shoulders. Amy loved to splash. Kneeling by the bathtub with my arms resting on its side, I wondered what the future would bring for this innocent child. I guess every parent has this thought. What have I brought this child into?

I heard Sarah turning the TV on as I dried Amy and myself. Powder, a quick diaper job and PJs completed my task. I placed my child in her crib tucking a light blanket around her. I joined Sarah on the couch to watch the evening news. Sure enough, I was the lead story. Again, no great surprise there. Pinhead, the vulture and the chief had held a news conference earlier. The news clip showed the chief at a podium speaking, "Officer Drake was terminated for breaking departmental policy. The Homicide Unit has completed their investigation, and the information has been turned over to the District Attorney's Office. No other comment will be made, and questions will not be entertained at this time because of the confidentiality of the matter being considered by the grand jury."

The chief backed away to stand next to the mayor. The vulture took the podium next. He had to adjust the microphone because there was a huge height discrepancy between him and the chief. I wondered if a box had been put behind the podium for him to stand on. He looked nervous. His eyes kept darting around the room.

Loudly clearing his throat, he said, "After consultation with Chief Hardesty and Mayor Michaels and reviewing the facts presented by the Homicide unit, I believe it is in the best interest of the citizens of this city to take this case to the grand jury."

A question was shouted from a reporter from behind the camera, "What will Drake be charged with?"

The vulture was clearly not prepared to be interrupted. He hesitated before answering, "Please hold your questions. The evidence will be presented to the grand jury, and they will decide whether Drake will be charged or not. Because the law doesn't allow any discussion of what is presented to the grand jury, I will not answer any further questions."

"Mumford was right," said Sarah sharply using two fingers signifying quotation marks. "He's not comfortable with taking it to the grand jury. He shared the blame with Hardesty and Michaels if it goes south."

The mayor shook hands with the DA as they swapped positions. Although the mayor had a smile on his face, his eyes revealed a different mood. He was clearly not pleased with the DA. His small head rotated making eye contact with the reporters before settling on the camera. He grasped the podium with both hands stooping to speak into the microphone rather than adjusting it.

The mayor waited until the murmurs stopped, "I feel that the police department through the able leadership of Chief Hardesty did an excellent job of investigating this incident. Once the facts were determined, as the law requires, they were turned over to the District Attorney's Office for review. The DA decided to present the evidence to the grand jury. I believe he made the right decision. A jury of the citizen's peers should make the decision if charges are to be made. As with the other gentlemen, it would be inappropriate for me to make any further comment."

"Talk about a Teflon coating," Sarah sarcastically commented. "He threw it back into the DA's lap. Nothing's going to stick to him. It was all the DA's decision. If that doesn't work, it was the jury's fault."

At the end of the newscast was an editorial comment section. These were becoming trendy. Not only did the news people determine what was newsworthy, they wanted to indoctrinate us as to why their viewpoint was correct. I should have known who would be the editorialist. Bellows appeared on the screen. He had a solemn expression. His backdrop was a gavel with "PERSONAL RESPONSIBILITY" printed in large blue letters.

Looking directly at the camera, he said, "As individuals, we are responsible for our actions. I make choices every day. If I make the wrong decision, then I suffer the consequences. Today, Chief Hardesty announced that John Drake was fired because he violated the department's policy for working an off duty job. Drake chose not to follow the department's *written* policy. The consequence of that decision was termination.

"Our DA is taking Drake's case to the grand jury. If Drake had followed departmental policy, permission to work at the bar would have been denied and the shooting wouldn't have taken place. Policies are put into place to avoid incidents such as this from arising. Drake has the right to appeal his termination. That's how the judicial system works.

"If the grand jury decides to indict, he has the right to a trial by a jury of his peers. Once again, that's how the judicial system works to assure equal justice for all. Where there's smoke, there must be fire; otherwise, the District Attorney would not take it to the grand jury. Regardless of the finding, two men are dead. Personal responsibility… We have nobody to blame but ourselves for our choices and our actions. John Drake must accept the responsibility for his choices. Jacob Bellows for Channel 12 news."

I didn't react to the editorial. I didn't feel anything. It was as if my nervous system had shut down. The body is an amazing machine; it knows how to compensate. My body knew I'd had enough stress for one day and was simply shutting down to eliminate the mental pain. I felt drained.

Sarah was angry. She jumped to her feet turning off the television with the remote, tossing it on the couch. I believe she would have clawed Bellows' eyes out if he were present. Looking at me, she said, "That son of a bitch! Talk about poisoning the well! How can you expect an unbiased jury with crap like that?"

Without waiting for an answer, she stormed to our bedroom. I heard her turn on the shower. I decided to let her calm down before talking to her. I retrieved the remote, turned on the television and changed to a different channel. I decided to watch our local educational channel. Mark Mumford was sitting at a table with several other people whom I assumed to be reporters. They were having a panel discussion.

Mumford was speaking, "I think you have to look at all the facts before deciding if Drake's termination was appropriate punishment for his infraction."

A young red headed man, who looked aggravated, opened his mouth to interrupt. Mumford held up a hand for the man to wait as he continued, "My station requested clarification about whether Officer Glass, who was killed, had submitted the proper form to work at the bar. Our request has been denied. The police department said it was part of his personnel file, and they do not release personal information. We also requested past actions taken for similar infractions. That request has been denied. We have filed suit under the freedom of information act."

"Nobody was killed even if there were other similar infractions," interrupted the red head. "You have to take into account the seriousness of this incident."

"Taking into account what you said," retorted Mumford. "If the other officer had permission, why wouldn't Drake have been given permission? Wouldn't he be working under de facto permission? You noted the seriousness of this incident. An officer doesn't know what is going to happen even with what we could consider the most minor incident. He makes a traffic stop for a violation. The driver tries to kill the officer. Go to the internet. You can download videos where a simple ticket turns into an explosive situation."

"Let's move to a different aspect of this case," injected the panel's moderator. The DA's Office is taking the case to the grand jury. Obviously, the DA believes he has enough evidence for a conviction. Our legal consultants indicate the charge will be either manslaughter or reckless homicide."

Mumford was the first to respond, "The grand jury is an antiquated system. Its origins date back to Assize of Clarendon in 1166. Less than half of the states use a grand jury because of the history of runaway grand juries. The progressive states have preliminary hearings. The evidence is presented to a judge. The judge decides if the prosecution can move forward. It's all in the open. There's no hiding behind closed doors."

"Which brings up another salient point," he continued. "How can we, as individuals, make a decision without the facts? Drake's case is being taken before the grand jury. There has been no indictment handed down. The jury could decide that he did nothing wrong under the circumstances.

Because the findings of a grand jury are held secret, we may never know all the facts. I'll report the facts and not speculate."

I had wearied of seeing my life dissected on television. I felt like life had been drained out of me. Depression would put it mildly. I turned the television off. I went to the bedroom to speak with Sarah. She was in her pajamas curled up in a fetal position on our bed. She was sobbing. I lay behind her draping an arm, holding her tightly. She choked the words out between sobs, "I don't want to lose you. They'll put you in prison. You'll be gone a long time. Amy won't know her father…"

Her sobbing intensified silencing any attempt to speak. I just held her. There was nothing I could say to alleviate her fears. I felt a pain in my chest for the sorrow I had caused her. I couldn't tell her that I was afraid too. I didn't want to go to prison. I didn't want to miss my child growing up. How much would prison change me? Would I even survive? What would I do when I got out? I silently cried with her. What did the fates have in mind for me?

***

Sleep. I don't think I actually slept last night. Dreams. Dreams are supposed to be the mind dumping garbage. Last night my mind was in hyper drive dumping garbage. I hovered between consciousness and sleep. The dreams were surreal. I was strapped on a gurney. Frank was standing over me holding a syringe. He wasn't talking, but I could hear his thoughts. I had killed him, and he was returning the favor. He was giving me a lethal injection because I had been found guilty. No matter how hard I struggled, the restraints dug into my skin holding me on the gurney. It was a relief to awake.

Sarah didn't look rested either. I helped her change the bed's sheets because I had soaked them with sweat. Neither of us brought up last night. I thought about the bond between Sarah and Amy. Then I thought about my mother. I hadn't seen or spoken with my mother long before the shooting. There was nothing wrong between us. Daughters keep in touch with their mothers after marriage. Sons drift away from their mothers after marriage. At least, that was the way it was with me.

I asked Sarah if she minded me visiting my mom. She thought it was a good idea. She mentioned that Mom had comment she hadn't heard from me. I guess Mom thought I had enough on my mind and didn't want to be a bother. She had one trait that every person should have. She was a listener. You could tell her anything, and she never passed judgment or breached confidentiality. I'm sure Dad had told her everything that had happened. Sarah had probably kept her informed.

My old junker's starter ground slowly as the car refused to start. It backfired finally coming to life. A light blue haze drifted down the driveway. On the drive to my parents' house, I admitted to myself that I really wanted to talk to Dad. I wanted his take on yesterday's news.

I parked in the drive and went to the back door which entered into their kitchen. Although I had a key to their house, I knocked on the door. Mom must have seen me walking down the driveway. She opened the door while I was still knocking. Mom was still a handsome woman. She didn't look 60. She could pass for being in her early fifties. She took care of herself. Her hair was expertly colored and styled. She constantly watched her diet.

She jogged everyday plus walked in the evening with Dad. They had walked together every evening since I was a kid. The walk was their time to catch up on the day's events. "I'm glad you came over, Johnny," Mom said with a pleasant smile. Mom never called me John. I'll always be Johnny to her. She had a simple philosophy: Once her child, always her child, no matter how old.

"Sorry I haven't been to see you," I said giving her a peck on the cheek.

"That's OK. You've had enough to deal with," she answered.

That was the way Mom was, gracious. She motioned me into the kitchen pouring a cup of coffee for me without asking. I sat at the table. Mom didn't say anything allowing me to decide what I wanted to say. She patted my hand then sat opposite me. She's a smart woman. Sometimes more can be said through silence than all the words in the world. I could feel her love for me.

She listened, occasionally asking a question to clarify something she didn't understand. She said Dad was having difficulty sleeping. He'd been out late at night several times. He was probably worrying about me. Mom told me she was concerned about him. Last night he had gotten up around midnight. He told her that he needed to get some fresh air and do some thinking. This type of behavior is unusual for my dad. He's not a night owl. I became concerned.

Both our concerns were temporarily alleviated when we heard whistling coming from the driveway. I swear, it sounded like "Hang on Sloopy". I knew it was a popular song from the sixties when Dad was in the military. I had another surprise when Dad entered the kitchen. He was dressed totally in black. He wore a long sleeve tee shirt and fatigue pants bloused in what I'd consider high top combat boots. He looked tired but had the spring in his step of a young man.

"Morning, John," Dad said as he entered the kitchen. "I'm glad you came by. I watched the news last night and couldn't sleep. Hell, I bet you didn't get much sleep either. Drove around most of the night thinking. It's going to get real nasty, but I think everything will work out OK. The average Joe doesn't know what this is really about. It's a skillful maneuver diverting attention from the mayor's track record. They're ignoring the fact that someone is trying to kill you. How many attempts until they're successful? I have to give it some more thought though."

The subject closed and wasn't brought back up. Dad's last comment shook me. I hadn't considered another attempt on my life. I thought they would back off. The police were in front of my house 24/7. Dad took a shower while Mom made him a light breakfast. He needed sleep so I didn't stay long. Mom had offered breakfast. I didn't feel like eating although I hadn't eaten today. My stomach would not tolerate anything solid. The last time I had weighed myself, I was still losing weight. Stress will do that to you. Dad had said he'd come over Sunday, after church and work on the deck.

I could count on one hand the number of Sundays Dad had missed a morning service. Going back to Sarah's theory of demons, Dad had demons of his own. He constantly battled them. I believe his demons stemmed from his tour of duty in Vietnam. I don't know what he did in Vietnam, but I think it left a gaping wound in his psyche. That wound never completely healed. The wound would fester, and he'd rely on his religion as a balm to sooth the pain. In my own way, I now understood.

When I got home, I saw an unmarked police car parked in front. What now? It was Detective Wilson. He had told Sarah that he had the day off and had come by to see how we were doing. He was dressed casually in a pull over shirt and blue jeans. I couldn't help noticing the large bulge on his belt under the shirt. Cops are supposed to carry their weapon 24/7. After some small talk, he asked me to walk out to his car with him. Leaning against car, he said, "Officially, as far as homicide is concerned, the case is closed. Unofficially, I'm keeping my file open."

"Ken, I appreciate your help," I said. "But, you're going to be in trouble if they find out."

"I don't know why, but I've got a gut feeling that this case is about to break wide open," he answered. "If there's one thing I've learned about this job, follow your gut feeling. It's seldom wrong. As far as the brass is concerned, I don't think there's a lot they can say. I'm a detective. I'm supposed to figure out the truth. If it doesn't detract from any of my other cases, what can they do? Transfer me back to the street? If they don't want the truth, then I'm in the wrong job."

***

I don't know what it was about this Saturday, but it turned out to be visitation day. What was I bitching about? I started the day with going to see my folks. My second visitor was Mark Mumford. He showed up at our home at six in the evening. Sarah was preparing a light supper. Neither of us was eating well. It's difficult to enjoy food in an emotional state.

Why did he come? He knew the ground rules. My anger showed when I answered the door because he held up a hand quickly saying, "I'm not here for an interview. As a matter of fact, I'd prefer nobody knew I came. Can I come in?"

I felt Sarah's presence before I heard her say, "John, invite Mr. Mumford in."

It was an order, not a request even if her voice was pleasant. In retrospect, I acted more like a sulking youth than an adult as I unblocked the doorway motioning him to follow. Sarah and I sat on the couch facing Mumford who sat on a recliner. He looked like he had just stepped off of a golf course. He wore a light green polo shirt with canary yellow slacks and tennis shoes. Obviously, he wasn't working today.

"I came by to pass along some information and to satisfy my curiosity," he said. "A source of mine says the forensics report definitely shows Officer Glass being shot from behind, but it presents some problems for the prosecution."

"You don't have to answer, but to satisfy my curiosity, how close were you to Officer Glass when he was shot?" he asked watching me.

I started not to answer but figured he knew the answer. He wanted confirmation. "Two feet behind him," I answered. "I took a step to his right before I shot."

Mumford said, "Now I understand why he said the prosecution had some problems. The report shows the bullet entered Glass's leg directly from behind, exiting the front at a 90 degree angle to the plane of his body. The path it traveled was almost parallel with the sidewalk if not slightly elevated from the back to the front. I'm not an expert, but if you had shot him, wouldn't the bullet have traveled at a 45 degree angle downwards?"

He was right! This could be information that would prove my innocence! I stood asking Mumford to stand facing me. I took a Weaver's stance as if I were holding a pistol. I took one step to the side so that I could see behind him. It was similar to Frank's and my positions, except Frank was facing away from me. I lowered my hands with the index fingers pointing like a gun barrel at Mumford's thigh. It was simple to see that the bullet's trajectory would have been a 45 degree angle downwards.

I could see what Mumford was saying. I pointed out another fact, "The bullet wouldn't have broken the body's plane at a 90 degree angle. It would have traveled closer to a 30 degree angle probably hitting the bone. The forensics report should clear me!"

"Not necessarily so," said Mumford shaking his head as he sat back down. "It's how the prosecution presents the evidence. There's no rebuttal at a grand jury. They could present it as if you were directly behind him squatted or on one knee. No witness has come forward to substantiate your testimony. They could say you're lying to cover yourself."

"Do you believe I'm lying?" I asked angrily.

"I wouldn't be here if I did," he responded calmly. "You're being screwed. You've got a good attorney. With this information, Henry Fellows can obtain expert witnesses for your defense in the trial. Yes, I said trial. As far as I'm concerned, the grand jury is a rubber stamp for the prosecution. A criminal trial is a different story. The prosecution has to convince the jury that you're guilty beyond a reasonable doubt."

"Even if John is exonerated, his name will be tainted," Sarah flared. "This will kill his career as a police officer. He'll be put in some do nothing job on third shift and forgotten."

"If he is found not guilty and if he decides to continue on the police force," answered Mumford with emphasis on the ifs, "memories fade. Administrations come and go. A new administration won't carry on this vendetta. They'll have other agendas."

"Which brings me to the other reason I came," Mumford continued. "I check my e-mail at the station several times a day, even when I'm off. Never know when something interesting will come in. I received a most interesting e-mail this afternoon with several pictures. We've both heard the rumors of the mayor's peculiar sexual preferences.

"The pictures are of our mayor in compromising positions with a male in the backseat of a limousine. The man appears to be very young. I'd say he was in his early teens. They're very graphic. I don't think they've been manipulated with a photo program. One picture is of the rear of the vehicle with the license plate. They're government plates. The pictures aren't great," he continued with a smirk. "I'd say they were taken using a camera equipped with night vision. I know my station will not run with this story. Probably sent them to a number of news agencies. Who knows where they were sent. Makes you wonder who got them?"

"Who sent them?" I asked with an image of Dad dressed in black and coming home from being out all night.

"No way to know," answered Mumford scrunching his eyebrows in thought. "It was a Yahoo account. The sender was identified as "Guardian_ of_ Justice_614". Anybody can open an e-mail account. If the sender has half a brain, it was sent from a coffee shop using their wireless network. The owner is untraceable unless you have the computer's signature ID number. Then again, so many laptops are resold or stolen that it's virtually impossible to trace the computer's owner."

"I see where you're going with this," Sarah said with the beginning of a smile curving the corners of her lips. "Some news agencies won't be as discerning as your station. It only takes one to break the story. The rest will jump on the band wagon. I understand why you said administrations come and go. If this story breaks, the mayor will have a hell of a time getting reelected."

"If one of the national rags gets the pictures, I'm positive they wouldn't hesitate running with the story," Mumford added with a thoughtful expression. "It would be national news. The network and cable news services would send reporters. His political opponent wouldn't have to say a word. It'd kill his creditability."

To his credit, Mumford didn't ask any other questions about the shooting. He didn't stay to make small talk. When he was finished, he politely bid his farewell. As I've said before, I think I have a touch of OCD. The last thing Mumford said before leaving kept replaying in my mind. He said, "To paraphrase Alice, this case gets curiouser and curiouser."

CHAPTER 12

True to his word, Dad was waiting for us when we got home from church. My folks went to early service while we prefer to sleep later and go to late service. He was dressed for work wearing a khaki shirt, blue jeans and scuffed boots with a baseball hat pulled down firmly over his eyes. I changed clothes as he hauled tools from his pickup truck to the backyard. Dad didn't believe in wasting time. He had set up his saw horses, plugged in his saw and was loading a nail gun as I came out of the house.

"You did a good job with the concrete," he said eyeing my work. "We should be able to get it framed with the joists in place by the end of the day. We may even get a few floor boards."

I didn't know how to approach Dad about the pictures even though I suspected he was responsible. I sure as hell wasn't going to accuse him of them. Alice was correct. Things just got curiouser and curiouser. I was curious, but I was cop. Better phrased, I had been a cop. As I've said before, cops are curious. I decided the best route was an indirect approach. I'd tell him about Mumford's visit.

I held the end of the tape as Dad measured for the first board. As he placed a square on the board to mark the cut, I said, "That reporter, Mark Mumford, came to the house yesterday."

"What'd he want?" he asked as he penciled a line across the board.

"He wanted to pass along some information," I answered. "The forensic report favors my version of the incident if I'm charged. Mumford thinks I'll be indicted, and he wanted me to give the information to my lawyer so he can get expert witnesses on my behalf."

"I'd say he has a good feel for the situation," Dad commented as he picked up the circular saw. The saw was loud, stopping our conversation as he cut the board.

"Mumford said he received some pictures," I said watching Dad's face for any change of expression as he put the saw on the ground. Dad didn't look at me or have any noticeable reaction. Since boyhood, I could never read him.

Dad didn't comment, so I continued, "He indicated the pictures showed the mayor having relations with a teenage boy. He didn't know who else got the pictures."

Dad stood, stretched, and arched his back. There were light popping sounds from vertebrae realigning. "Getting old is hell," he said with a scowl. "I'd say the mayor has a whole heap of trouble heading his way. He sure pissed somebody off. You don't kick a bull in the ass if you're not willing to deal with the horns."

I swear I thought I saw a twinkle in Dad's eyes that left as quick as it appeared. Dad lifted his end of the board nodding for me to get the other end. The subject was closed to further discussion. There's an old saying that you can't hang a man for what he thinks. Dad took that expression one step further. You can't put your foot into your mouth if you don't open your mouth. Those two phrases summed up Dad. Seldom, if ever, would he give an opinion, even when asked.

We fell into our familiar routine when working together. Talk was held to needs of the job. Both men lost in their own thoughts yet aware of the presence of the other. After the frame was completed and the joists placed one at a time, I understood why Dad liked building. I stood with my hands on my hips pleased with our progress. My stomach protested loudly when I smelled the aroma of food being cooked, drifting out the kitchen window. I hadn't eaten since breakfast. I glanced at my watch. It was 5:30 P.M. Where had the day gone?

Dad stored his tools in my garage. No need to take them with him. He'd be back in the morning to finish the deck. He refused to stay saying Mom was holding supper. Sarah gave him a hug, and Amy squealed when he playfully rubbed his facial stubble against her cheek. Sarah had to pry Amy's arms off him. It was playtime with Grandpa as far as Amy was

117

concerned. Dad kissed her on the forehead as Sarah withdrew the protesting toddler.

Sarah had prepared homemade vegetable soup with ham sandwiches. I ate a sandwich and a small bowl of soup. The soup was delicious, but I didn't want to overtax my somewhat fitful stomach. After helping to clean the kitchen, Sarah said she had something to show me. She put Amy in her playpen with a few toys. She brought the laptop to the kitchen connecting to the internet.

"While Dad and you were working, I surfed the net to see what I could find on Michaels," she informed me with a smirk. "You're the least of his troubles."

She had several sites bookmarked so she could easily navigate to them. I was surprised... No, I was shocked by the first site she had on the screen. It was a porn site. With a few mouse clicks, the screen was filled with pictures of Mayor Michaels with a boy performing fellatio on him. You couldn't see the boy's face. Whoever had taken the picture was careful with the angle to shield the boy's identity. There was no mistaking Michaels' face.

Michaels was leaned back in the driver's seat with the boy's face buried in his lap. The mayor had his eyes closed clearly enjoying himself. "It's disgusting, isn't it?" asked Sarah continuing before I had a chance to answer. "It was submitted as an amateur photo to the porn site. It lists the date and time it was submitted, yesterday at three. It lists the sender as Guardian_of_Justice_614. Whoever it is, he's been busy."

Without waiting, she brought up another site. This was a gay blog site. It proclaimed that it was about time Mayor Michaels came out of the closet. The site included a disclaimer about sex with a minor. I figure they were covering their ass legally. It'd put them in a bind with the authorities if they promoted sex with underage participants.

What would the crimes against children unit think of these pictures? Did "Guardian" e-mail them to the police? Would Chief Hardesty try to cover it up? As Dad said, they had a whole heap of trouble heading their way!

The next site was an investigative news ezine. It was strictly an internet magazine claiming to be the first to break headline news. It was probably one person working from a computer at home. Most of the articles looked like old news to me with the exception of one headline. It screamed in large red letters: "Mayor of major city caught in sex scandal!" It had the pictures; however, the boy's face had been made into a smear to make his features totally unrecognizable. Turning the computer off, Sarah quipped, "I thought "Mayor caught with his pants down!" would be more appropriate."

"I suspect the printed investigative rags have the pictures too," Sarah said as she closed the top. "Even if they don't, I'm sure the other internet magazines look at their competition's sites. This is going to spread like wildfire."

***

Monday started out routine. I had breakfast with the family. Sarah took Amy to Mom before going to work. It felt strange not having a job, not having a specific place to report. Was this what retirement felt like, with the exception of not having any money coming in to pay the bills? Thank God Sarah had a job. It's hard to describe, but I felt like less of a man. Logically, I knew there was nothing I could do about the situation. Too many factors were undecided for me to make a decision for my future.

The OCD started to invade my thought process. Sure, Fellows said he could get my job back at the department, but that was before it was announced I was going to be indicted. If I was charged, then Fellows would have to defend me at a trial before appealing my firing. If I was found guilty, then I'd go to jail and never be re-instated. Police departments don't hire ex cons. I wouldn't have the right to carry a gun or vote. I'd have a hell of a time finding employment. Employers shy away from ex cons. It's a matter of trust. It's hard to trust a person who has been in jail for murder.

OCD is a strange illness. It's like a loop on a tape player. The same thoughts keep playing over and over. I always thought I had a touch of OCD, but it was getting worse. Was it the stress activating it? I had to get busy. Focus on something else to shove these thoughts out of my mind. I could create a hundred scenarios. The truth was that I didn't know what would happen. I went outside and was opening the garage when I saw Dad's truck in the driveway.

He slapped a pair of leather gloves against his thigh as he walked to me. "Have you listened to the news?" he asked with an angry expression.

"No," I answered.

"That son of a bitch Durbin announced he was convening a grand jury for your case today," he hissed!

He clenched his jaws as if he wanted to say something else but thought better of it. "Nothing I can do about it," I said as a sickening feeling rose in my stomach. "Let's get to work, Get our minds off of it."

He nodded in resignation abruptly turning to pick up the saw horses. Again, we fell into our routine of silently working. I tried to focus on working, but the loop kept playing in my mind. I wondered if Sarah had heard the news. If Dad had, then she probably had. How would it affect her? It couldn't be good. We were trying to put our lives back together. This could rip us apart again.

***

We nailed the last plank into place as the sun was in its arc downward surrendering to darkness. Sarah was in the kitchen frying chicken. I could tell she was upset when she arrived home, but she had held her emotions in check, mainly for my benefit. Dad had made himself scarce allowing us privacy to talk. We didn't talk much. We mostly held each other. I swear that I felt some of her strength and resolve flow into me. In ways, she's stronger than I.

Dad was shaking the sawdust out of his circular saw when two marked units parked in front of our house. Dad and I saw them at the same time. He walked to stand beside me as four uniforms exited the cars. Neither of us spoke as the officers approached us. One officer had several sheets of paper in his hand. It had to be an arrest warrant. I started to panic. I didn't want to be caged like an animal.

Dad gently placed a hand on my shoulder saying, "Don't John. It'll make it worse."

I didn't know any of the officers. I may have seen them around the precinct, but I didn't know them personally. I could tell by their body language that they didn't like what they had to do. The officer with the paperwork stood facing me while one went to each side of us with the last officer circling to the rear. I knew what they were doing. We call it contact and cover. The officer facing me would speak to me. The others would cover him in case a physical altercation took place.

"Sir," he said addressing my dad. "Please go sit on the deck."

Dad's eyes blazed as he slowly backed away towards the deck. Sarah ran out the rear door screaming, "John, what's going on?"

Dad moved like an agile cat springing to the deck holding her back. I heard her hysterically screaming for him to let go. Her screams became wails of sorrow as Dad held her. She collapsed into his arms as he cradled her head to his chest. The lead officer looked like he was going to be sick. He took a deep breath before asking, "You're John Drake, correct?"

"I'm John Drake," I answered steeling myself.

"I have a warrant for your arrest. The charge is reckless homicide. Put your hands behind you back."

I straightened my back placing both hands behind my back, palms facing outward, and thumbs up. I knew the routine. I had been a cop. I felt the cold steel bite into my flesh as the cuffs were snapped on my wrists. I felt the officer check each cuff to assure blood circulation wasn't cut off before securing the locking mechanism. Now I knew how those I had arrested must have felt. It is embarrassing and degrading. All freedom is instantly gone.

I was frisked for weapons. It was nothing against me. It was a safety precaution. If a weapon was found, a second, more intense search would be conducted since there was a very high probability that the suspect had a second weapon somewhere on his person. That was a proven fact. Weapons had been found stashed in the rear seat of cruisers where officers had missed them. It was standard procedure to check the back seat before starting the booking process.

I had nothing on my person except a wrist watch. I asked the officer to give it to Sarah knowing I wouldn't be allowed to keep it in jail. It had a strap so he didn't have to remove a cuff to get it off. He gave the watch to her. She stood beside my Dad. Her cheeks were covered with black streaks from her mascara.

News reporters were clustered in the road. They had to have been tipped off to be here so quickly. Bellows was standing in front of a camera speaking into a microphone. The camera was strategically placed to use my arrest as background. I spotted Mumford. He was silently standing beside a cameraman who was filming my arrest.

The officers formed a phalanx around me walking towards their cruisers. Anger welled up inside me. I wasn't guilty. I wasn't going to act the part. We've all seen the clips of prisoners trying to hide their identities with their heads bowed to conceal their faces. Others ask to have their shirts pulled up over their faces or have a jacket draped over their heads. Damnit, I wasn't guilty! I didn't need to be ashamed.

Squaring my shoulders, I held my head high staring straight ahead. Bellows had a smirk as if he thought it was funny. Mumford was frowning at the travesty unfolding before him. The other reporters' faces blurred as they jockeyed for position to either snap a picture or get a film clip. The officers closed ranks around me as we approached the cruiser. The lead officer broke ranks quickly opening the rear door as I felt a hand on top of my head pushing me down to avoid striking my head.

The officer who had been on my right leaned over me fastening the seatbelt while reporters shouted questions. All the officers' faces were expressionless as they ignored the reporters. The door slammed locking me in the cage. The backseat of police cars are effectively a cage. A shield divides the rear occupants from the front seat, and the rear inside door release is disabled.

Two officers slid into the front compartment slamming their doors. I heard the passenger mumble to the driver, "Sometimes I hate this fucking job!"

Neither officer said anything else until we were well away from the reporters. Without taking his eyes off the road, the driver used his right hand to slide open the shield's center window. I could see his eyes watching me in the rearview mirror as he said, "I didn't volunteer for this shit detail. The LT asked for volunteers. Nobody came forward. I was one of the unfortunate ones who got picked."

"Same with me," said the passenger. "I tried to get out of it, but the LT told me he didn't like it anymore than I did. Just get my ass in gear and my job."

It was as close as they could come to apologizing for arresting me. The police are part of the executive branch of government. They carry out the laws passed by the legislature. The executive branch, which prosecutors are part of, determines how to carry out the law. If given a lawful order, then the police must obey. An arrest warrant is a lawful written order. The officers had no choice but to enforce the warrant.

The driver and I kept eye contact using the rearview mirror. "I understand," I said. "I would have done the same thing if our roles were reversed."

"I think you're getting a raw deal," said the passenger which garnered a dirty look from the driver.

Ignoring the driver, he continued, "It could be any one of us under the right circumstances. Absolutely no fucking support from Michaels or Hardesty. I don't believe you shot Glass. It doesn't make sense from what I've heard. I think something's missing, and they haven't dug deep enough. It makes you leery of pulling your weapon. Some cop's going to get hurt because he hesitates to think about whether he'll have a job or be thrown to the wolves."

I felt the car accelerate. I think the driver was uncomfortable with the conversation and wanted to get to Corrections. Corrections is the politically correct euphemism for jail. Society doesn't like to think we put people behind bars for punishment. A criminal is a criminal. Yes, we put them in small cages so they can learn not to do it again, thus the term Corrections. It must be a throwback to the flower children. We're all supposed to sit around a campfire singing kumbayah. If it walks like a duck, quacks like a duck...

The driver pulled the marked unit into the entrance of Correction's sally port. There are two large metal overhead doors which are kept closed. They are supposed to be opened only to allow entrance. A camera is mounted so the corrections officers can see the entrance. The interior is like a large concrete block garage, big enough to park four semi tractors and trailers. There's another set of overhead doors for exiting sally port. Those doors are supposed to be closed except for allowing a vehicle to exit.

There have been a few exceptions to the rule. During the height of summer, the interior gets very hot. Sometimes, even though it's against procedure, the doors are left open because the air conditioning is undersized and can't handle the high temperature. Prisoners are supposed to be chained to anchored benches against the right side of sally port. If prisoners seem civil, although they are still in handcuffs, sometimes the cops don't chain them to the benches because it's highly uncomfortable.

I don't know if it's a scientific law or what, but if something can go wrong, it usually does. One summer day, when the weather was sweltering, it happened. The doors were all open. Most of the prisoners waiting to be booked weren't chained to the bench. There was a mass break for freedom. I don't know where the prisoners thought they were going. They were handcuffed. Imagine the keystone cops. Prisoners handcuffed running down city streets with cops and correction officers in pursuit. Pretty funny if you've got a sense of humor.

The overhead door groaned as it opened. How many thousand times has it opened? Sally port was crowded. It's always crowded in the evening hours until the wee hours of morning. The officer on the passenger side helped me out of the rear seat as the driver came around the front of the car with the paperwork. They didn't chain me to the bench but led me directly to the booking door. Normally, officers waited their turn to book prisoners, first come, first served sort of deal.

There were a few catcalls from the benches when some of the prisoners recognized me. Even criminals watch the news. Some of them even read the newspaper. I don't know which, but one of the prisoners yelled, "Good luck on the inside, fuckin' pig!"

The chatter abruptly ended when a group of officers went to the benches. A large corrections officer came out the booking area slipping on a pair of blue vinyl gloves. His shaved head reflected the light like a polished car reflects sunlight. "This is Officer Drake?" he asked.

"John Drake," the driver answered with a mild hint of reproach in his voice. It was obvious. In his opinion, I was no longer an officer, even if I were innocent. I was a prisoner. I understood the looks thrown at the other officer.

"John," said the corrections officer blowing the driver off. "You know the routine. Any weapons or drugs on you?"

"No sir," I answered.

"Take the cuffs off. Give me his paperwork. He's in my custody," ordered the corrections officer. It was his way of telling the driver that he didn't appreciate the attitude. The cop was on his turf now. He could keep his attitude in check.

He signaled the officer in the control room. The solenoid on the metal booking room door buzzed as it unlocked. He guided me to a wall with a white backdrop. "I don't like this anymore than you do. I think you're getting screwed. OK? I have to search you. It's humiliating, but I can't make exceptions. Put your hands above your head and on the wall. Spread you legs.

He was correct. It was humiliating. He explored every crevice of my body. He looked in my mouth to see if I was hiding anything under my tongue or in my checks. He took me though a metal detector to another area where I was electronically finger printed and photographed. Required paperwork was filled out such as personal data, personal property, an identification number and medical information. My clothes were exchanged for a bright orange jumpsuit. I was given a storage bag to take with me. Different colored jump suits signify the prisoner's status. The bright orange is used for prisoners placed in protective custody. The prisoner is placed in a cell by himself. Two corrections officers must accompany the prisoner during movement.

I was handed over to two other officers who guided me through a maze of hallways. Each hallway had an electronic door. One of the officers waited until we couldn't be overheard, "We were given a heads up you were coming in. It's totally bullshit. We're taking you to segregation confinement, out of the general population.

"You'll be arraigned tomorrow morning. If there's any way possible, make bail and get out of here. We can only do so much. Somebody will finger you as a cop. The least you can expect would be to get the hell beat out of you. Eventually, one of these assholes will figure out a way to stick a shank between your ribs. I can guarantee that none of the inmates will have seen anything."

I was searched again before I was put in a jail cell I guessed to be 6 foot by 8 foot. There's no expressing the feeling when the steel door swings shut. You're totally enclosed with only a window in the door to look out. No inside handle on the door with a heavy duty steel lock only accessible from the outside. There was a single steel frame bed attached to the floor and wall with a thin mattress and pillow. A stainless steel toilet and sink were attached to the opposite wall.

I emptied my storage bag on the bed. It contained a set of sheets, pillowcase, towel, blanket, roll of toilet paper and hygiene materials. I sat on the bed cradling my face in my hands. I felt numb. It had to be a nightmare. Was this the way I was going to spend the rest of my life? I tried to fight back the tears forming in my eyes. I couldn't show weakness in this place. It didn't work. My hands became drenched from tears as my soul was ripped apart.

I heard something metallic knocking on the door. I grabbed the towel wiping my face. I didn't want anybody seeing me cry. The towel was fouled with dirt. I wasn't given a chance to clean up before I was arrested. I saw the corrections officer peering through the door's window. His muffled voice said, "I got you something to eat. It's not much, but it'll have to do. The prisoners call it a Z bowl. The term's a hangover from the old days when the Zeta Company prepared meals for the prisoners. Now the meals are prepared in-house by inmates."

A slit in the door slid open with a tray sliding through. I took the tray and set it on the bed. I should have thanked the officer, but I was afraid of my voice would crack. It was a kind gesture. There was a sandwich, an apple and two small cartons of milk. I felt grimy. I stripped all my clothes off pitching them on the bed. It didn't matter if I was naked. Nobody could see me.

Adjusting the flow of water in the sink until I had a warm stream, I fetched the bar of soap given to me to clean my face, hair, hands and arms. It was awkward, but I managed to get one foot at a time in the sink to rinse them. I used one end of the towel as a make shift face cloth to clean the rest of my body. The remaining part of the towel somewhat dried my hair and body. My hair was extremely short so I didn't have to bother with it.

Folding the towel neatly, I hung it from the bowl of the sink. In a sense, it put some order into my life. It was a little thing, but it seemed significant to me. Everything of value in my life had been ripped from me. The few items in the room were all I had now. I don't know why, but it became important to put things away in an orderly fashion. After I dressed, I made the bed squaring the corners in military fashion with the blanket tightly tucked. I neatly repacked all the other items in the storage bag placing it under the bed.

I sat on the bed feeling depleted and spaced out. I took the wrapping off the sandwich. It was ham and cheese. My stomach felt queasy. I ate a bite chewing it slowly. I opened one of the cartons of milk from the tray and took a sip. It was between warm and cool. I took a bite of sandwich, then a sip of milk, everything in an orderly fashion. It was the only way I could maintain my sanity. I had to have some control of my life.

It took me a half hour to finish eating. I didn't think about anything as if I were a zombie going through the motions. Leaving the apple, I put the tray on the sink before getting to bed pulling the sheet and blanket over my head. I tried to block out the light. I had no idea when the lights would be turned off or at least dimmed. Sleep didn't come easily. I could hear yelling from the other cells. Didn't these people ever sleep? The loop of the events of the day kept playing in my head. Mercifully, I drifted into a restless sleep.

CHAPTER 13

I don't know what time the lights were turned on, but it was damn early. A corrections officer told me it was 4 A.M. Breakfast was shoved through the slit again. It was scrambled eggs, toast and something indescribable which I think was gravy along with the two cartons of milk. I ate the toast, picked at the eggs and drank one carton of milk. I was given a disposable plastic razor which I had to return as soon as I finished shaving. I brushed my teeth with one thought on my mind. When would I be arraigned?

I paced the cell like a lion burning up nervous energy. To keep my mind occupied, I counted the paces. I stopped counting after a 1,000. An eternity passed before I heard a knocking on the cell door. I was instructed to put my hands through the slot. When I did, a set of handcuffs were snapped on my wrists. Next, I was ordered to step away from the door. The officer watched me through the window. It was 5 A.M. I was being transferred to the Hall of Justice where court was held.

There was the unmistakable sound of a key unlocking the door. The door swung open. The officer motioned for me to come out of the cell. He and another officer took me to the end of the hall. Prisoners screamed obscenities as we passed their cells. The officers ignored the taunting. An electronic door had to be unlocked for us to proceed. We traveled through several hallways until we reached an exit door.

The exit door led to an enclosed catwalk to the Hall of Justice. The Hall of Justice was a long walk way with a series of holding cells. It was out of sight from the public and court rooms. It originally got its name because prisoners were lined in the hall before going to court to receive justice. I was given into the custody of a deputy sheriff once we were inside the courthouse. I was searched by the deputy. Every time I turned around, I was searched. Again, I was placed in a holding cell by myself.

The holding cell was a replica of my other cell with a bench instead of a bed. I sat on the bench waiting. I was surprised when the deputy came to my cell informing me that my attorney wanted to speak to me. I was escorted to a room with a window separating me from Fellows who was in an adjoining room which one entered from the court room side. We could speak to each other, but there could be no physical contact.

Fellows was visibly agitated. "Your wife contacted me last night," he said. "The DA should have had the courtesy to notify me of the warrant. I could have arranged for you to surrender your person along with making arrangement for arraignment. You're at the front of the docket. You'll be brought in front of the judge. The charges will be read. They'll ask for your plea. You'll plead not guilty. I'll handle it from there."

He paused for a moment marshalling his thoughts before speaking. "I'm going to ask for release on your own recognizance. I don't know if the judge will go along with it. It probably won't happen. The prosecutor is going to argue for no release. Since there's been so damn much publicity, the judge might require a cash bond to cover her ass. She's an elected official. She doesn't want any blowback. We'll cross that bridge when we come to it."

The deputy knocked on the outside window interrupting us saying, "He's next on the docket. I'm going to take him to the courtroom."

Fellows stood knocking on the door for the deputy to let him out. A deputy let me out of the cell and did the mandatory search of my body. Anytime a prisoner is moved, he is searched. Fellows was let out of his cell into the court room while I was kept in the secure area. The deputy led me to another locked door. I could see the court room through the door's window.

The deputy said, "The judge doesn't want defendants in handcuffs in the courtroom. I don't agree with her, but it's her courtroom. We do what we're ordered. There have been a couple of brawls in the courtroom because of her policy. We've been fortunate so far. Nobody's escaped or gotten to the judge. Let one go over the bench. She'll change her tune."

It's amazing how many fights break out in a court room or outside of the court room in the public halls. Family members in the observation section, infuriated with the defendant, jump the banister and physically attack the defendant. Defendants, who are angry about their sentence, attack their attorneys, or the defendant tries to attack the judge. Two groups may decide to physically settle their differences in the hall outside of the court room. It can be a zoo.

The deputy took a long shank handcuff key from his shirt pocket. As he unlocked the cuffs, he eyes kept glancing at my face. As the first cuff snapped open, he said in a low voice, "You're still a cop as far as I'm concerned."

He hadn't said much, but those few words let me know how most officers felt. It gave me hope. He signaled another deputy in the courtroom as he unlocked the door. The courtroom deputy took my arm and said, "Stand behind the podium. Don't speak unless spoken to."

Fellows stood behind the podium with a second deputy to his right. I scanned the gallery seeing Sarah with Amy, Dad and Mom in the front row. They looked physically depleted except for Amy. The toddler sucked her thumb as her head swiveled trying to take everything in. The gallery was packed. Two more deputies stood in front of the gallery with another deputy stationed to the right of the judge's bench. I knew why there were so many deputies in the courtroom. It was a high profile case. Many of the people attending the arraignment were reporters. I saw people with notebooks. Pencils and pens were poised to record the event.

I was placed beside Fellows with the deputy to my left. The judge was younger than I expected. She looked to be in her mid thirties with long blond hair reaching over the collar of her black robe. The dark red lipstick accented her thin pale features, but her blue eyes gave me chills. Eyes are the windows to the soul. Her eyes were cold as she examined me like a pathologist looking at a tissue sample. There would be no mercy given.

"Your Honor," said Fellows. "Henry Fellows here, representing John Drake."

"I am aware, thank you," she answered turning her head to look at the prosecution. "Please read the charge Mr. Prosecutor."

The prosecutor, who was sitting at a table to our left, stood looking down at a legal pad on the table. It was not the DA, John Durbin, but was a heavy set man in black framed glasses whose hair had the beginning streaks of grey. Fellows was correct. The DA had handed the case off to an assistant. Looking at the judge, the Assistant DA said, "The state charges Mr. John Drake with reckless homicide."

"How do you plea, Mr. Drake?" asked the judge formally.

Fellows leaned close and whispered into my ear, "Not guilty, Your Honor."

"Not guilty, Your Honor," I answered louder than I meant to speak.

"What does the prosecution recommend for bail?" she asked.

The ADA pushed the large framed glasses back up his nose before answering, "The prosecution recommends Mr. Drake be held without bail. We feel that he is a flight risk."

"Your Honor, if I may address the bench?" asked Fellows.

"Please do," the judge answered.

"It's absurd to insinuate that Mr. Drake is a flight risk," Fellows said with a subtle sarcasm. "He has a wife, young child and owns a residence. I recommend he be released on his own recognizance. He was a police officer, and I believe he will be reinstated after the trial."

"Objection, Your Honor!" shouted the ADA. "Mr. Fellows is clouding the issue. I agree Mr. Drake *was* a police officer with emphasis on *was*. We are here because he is charged with reckless homicide! We are *not* here to determine if he will be reinstated as a police officer! Mr. Fellows' last statement shouldn't be taken into consideration."

"Objection sustained," ruled the judge turning her focus from the ADA to Fellows. "I agree that he was a police officer, but please keep your opinions about future litigation to yourself, Mr. Fellows."

Fellows didn't appear to be cowed by her admonishment. Whether the objection was sustained or not, he made two points in public. First, he as much said he would win the trial. Second, he believed I would be reinstated. He had slapped the DA, mayor and police chief with an invisible glove in rebuttal to their challenge.

The courtroom was silent as the judge wrote on a piece of paper. When she was finished, she laid the pen to the side of the bench and said, "Because of the uniqueness of this case, I will not release the defendant on his own recognizance. Nor, will I hold him without bail. Bail is set at $50,000 full cash bond."

My hope crashed to the floor. I couldn't look up as the deputy guided me back to the holding cell. Sarah and I didn't have that sum of money.

131

Our parents weren't rich. I didn't think either set had that much cash set aside. I'd have to stay in jail until the trial. With all the procedural jockeying, there was no telling how long I'd be in jail. How long could the jail keep me in segregation? What would happen when I was moved to the general population? I might not live long enough to have a trial!

I was not taken back to the holding cell in the courthouse but was taken to my cell in the corrections facility. I was so sick in my stomach that I heaved what was left of the content from breakfast into the small sink. I didn't touch lunch asking the officer to take it away when it was offered. I thought about killing myself, but the cell didn't lend itself to accomplish the task. I'm sure its designers took that aspect into account.

I sat on the side of the bunk abjectly miserable staring at my feet. I don't know how long I had been in a trance when I heard a key turning in the lock. The metal door swung open revealing two correction officers blocking the doorway. One of them said, "Your bail's been posted."

I couldn't believe what I was hearing. Who had enough money to make bail? After I was out processed, I was led to the front lobby of the facility. My dad was standing by the large plate glass windows waiting for me. He held his hand up for me not to speak. "We'll talk outside," he said as I followed him through the door.

Once we were on the sidewalk, he said, "Mom and I had a CD that wasn't drawing much interest. We felt it was a better investment getting you out of that place."

"I can't express how appreciative I am," I said. I don't know what was with me lately. The faucets turned on. Tears were dripping off my cheeks. I had no control over my emotions. I was a train wreck. Dad moved beside me half patting and half rubbing my back as we walked.

"Nothing wrong with crying," he said watching me from the corner of his eyes. "It's the soul's way of unburdening itself of sadness or sharing joy. Doesn't make you any less of a man."

His jaw flexed as he considered whether he wanted to continue this line of conversation or not before saying, "When I killed my first man in Nam, I cried. What was a young boy 18 years old from Kentucky doing in the jungle killing people? Each time I squeezed the trigger, my soul screamed in revulsion. I kept it bottled inside of me. I rationalized I was a warrior. I was a soldier. I was following orders. I didn't want to admit I thought I had lost my salvation."

Tears were forming in his eyes as he continued, "When I came home, I was very ill. I checked into the VA hospital. Half my stomach was removed because of ulceration. Today, they call it Post Traumatic Stress Syndrome. I kept losing weight. I was dying. The doctors had given up on me. They couldn't figure out what was wrong. Your mother was a floor nurse there. She'd just graduated from nursing school. She's a smart woman. She knew what was wrong with me."

He paused pulling out a handkerchief dabbing at his eyes before loudly blowing his nose and continuing, "One morning, she brought a young preacher to my room. I didn't want to talk with him, but she insisted. The preacher explained to me that God was a God of many hearts. There's a time for peace, and there's a time for war. There have to be warriors to protect God's children. God understands. I hadn't lost my salvation. It wasn't long before I checked out of the VA. I married that young nurse."

"Who was the preacher?" I asked.

"Don't interrupt me, boy," Dad answered now smiling. "You've known him all your life. He's the pastor of our church. Brother Johnny, your name sake, had just graduated from the seminary. He hadn't been called to a church. Me and five other veterans got together and bought a piece of land. We built a small church on the land for Brother Johnny. We only had hand tools. Glad I was young. I couldn't work like that today. I discovered I like building things. I went into construction. Haven't regretted it a day."

Dad actually laughed, "The first service had maybe 20 people in attendance. Now look at it. Thousands attend service every Sunday. People make fun of it because it's so large. They've even tagged it with theme park names. Nothing wrong with that. Jesus would want people enjoying church. I've come the long way to make my point. You've done nothing wrong. God has to have warriors protecting his people. He'll protect you. It'll all work out OK in the end. He has plans. We just don't know His plans until He chooses to reveal them."

***

Dad's sharing helped ease the burden. I'm not saying I wasn't still worried, but I regained hope. I actually felt hungry. Dad sprung for lunch.

He had to. I didn't have any money on me. I made a pig out of myself. After 3 hamburgers, fries and a chocolate milkshake, I rode home content. I was asleep when we arrived at my house. Dad tapped the horn telling Sarah we were there. She came running out the front door. I sprang out of the truck meeting her halfway. I kissed her as I picked her up off her feet in a hug.

Dad sauntered over to us giving us time. Sarah hugged him, thanking him. After we all settled down, Sarah said, "I took the day off because Dad told me he was going to post bail. Amy's asleep in the crib. A little bird named Mumford called me. He gave me a website to look at. Come into the house. I want to show both of you something."

The laptop was sitting on the kitchen table with the lid open. She made a few keystrokes pulling up a website where people can post video clips. The clip's title was: "Newsman makes a goof". The video showed Jacob Bellows with the Channel 12 logo behind him."

It was obvious that Bellows thought he was off the air. He was unclipping a small microphone off of his shirt collar. A voice from off camera asked, "Do you really believe Drake is guilty?"

"Hell yes," Bellows said in a snarl. "The son of a bitch shot both those guys and didn't give a second thought about it. I hope they hang him out to dry."

The screen went blank for a second. When it came back on, the Channel 12 logo with the words "technical difficulties please stay tuned" printed over the logo filled the screen.

"Mumford said there was a huge screw up," Sarah informed us. "Bellows and whoever he was talking to thought he was off the air. There's supposed to be a 10 second delay switch to cut out things like this from being broadcast. Somebody was asleep at the wheel."

"I'd say Channel 12 has troubles. They've just prejudiced the local jury pool," commented Dad thoughtfully scratching his chin.

"Henry Fellows is all over it," Sarah said. "He's been on television saying John can't get a fair trial. He said he's going to file a motion for a change of venue. Also, he said it was libel. I think we'll be hearing from him. Channel 12 has broadcast a statement denying responsibility for Bellows' statement. They said Bellow's been suspended pending an internal investigation. The other stations aren't showing the clip, but they keep replaying Fellows' statement."

The phone rang interrupting our conversation. The caller ID showed it was from Fellows' law office. Sarah handed the phone to me. When I answered, Fellows said, "John, is that you?"

"Yes, Dad bailed me out this morning," I said.

"Good, good. I went over to Corrections to talk with you. They said your bond was posted, so I called your house. I guess you know what happened on Channel 12?" he asked.

"Yes, Sarah told me," I informed him.

"I need your permission to do two things. I want to file for a change of venue. I believe your case has been prejudiced, and you can't get a fair trial locally. I want to immediately file a suit against Channel 12 and against Jacob Bellows, personally, for libel.

"Before I pursue this matter, I need to come to an agreement with you about fees. Because I feel you have a strong case against Channel 12, I'm prepared to handle the case without an hourly fee. If we receive any compensation, I'll take one third as my fee. If there's no compensation, then I get nothing," he said rapidly.

"Sir, do what you think is best," I answered.

"Very good," he answered hanging up.

"That was quick," I said to nobody in particular staring at the phone.

I pushed the end button on the phone starting to lay it on the table when it rang again. It was Detective Wilson. He said he'd be at our house in ten minutes. He told me to be dressed and ready to go with him. Curtly he hung up without waiting for an answer.

None of us could figure out what Wilson was up to. We didn't think he was going to arrest me. I'd just got out of jail. Dad agreed to stay with Sarah until I returned. The butterflies returned to my stomach as I went to our bedroom to change clothes. Sarah followed me. She looked somewhere between worried and perplexed. I didn't think it would help to speculate so I didn't say anything. I held her in my arms for a moment before changing.

Wilson was knocking on our front door before the ten minutes were up. He asked me to go with him with no explanation. Once we were in his car backing out of the driveway, he said, "I got a call from the hospital. It took me a while to track you down. I'm glad you're out. It'd have complicated matters if you were still in jail."

135

CHAPTER 14

Wilson was in a hurry to get to wherever we were going pushing the unmarked unit well above the posted speed. He glanced at me as he said, "Brandy, Janice, whatever her name is, apparently is going to make it. She's come out of her coma and is off the respirator. Nobody else knows. I don't want anybody getting to her before I do or should I say we do. She wants to talk but has the same stipulation. She'll only talk to you. I've got a gut feeling about what she knows."

Wilson didn't volunteer any more information. I wasn't in a position to ask. He seemed to know where he was going when we entered the hospital. We took the elevator to the ninth floor. There was a sign stating we were in the intensive care unit. A locked glass door barred entrance into the unit. There was a speaker with a button mounted beside the door. After Wilson pushed the button, a woman's voice asked us what we needed. Wilson identified himself as a police officer. The solenoid buzzed unlocking the door for us.

He went directly to the nurse's station asking a woman who appeared to be in charge, "Which room is the Jane Doe in?"

"I'm Dr. Williams," the woman said. "May I see some identification?"

Wilson removed a badge case from the inside of his suit pocket holding it open directly in front of the doctor's face. The doctor compared the picture ID to Wilson satisfying herself that he was indeed a police officer. She kept glancing at me. I didn't know if she expected me to produce some ID or recognized me from the news. She didn't ask. I didn't volunteer.

Addressing Wilson, the doctor said, "She's still in critical condition. Don't stay very long."

"Would you mind going with us?" asked Wilson.

The doctor shrugged her shoulders as if saying she had nothing else pressing. She led us to a room which had a pink index card in a holder beside the door. Alice Johns was hand printed on the card. When the hospital didn't know a patient's identity, an alias is assigned. Janice was now Alice. It struck me odd. Every time I met the woman, she was using a different name. How many names has she had?

I hardly recognized her. Most of her face was a yellow green from bruising. The top of her head was wrapped in a dressing. I think her head had been shaved. Tubes were sticking out of her body going to various machines. A television hung on the wall was on a local channel with the volume turned low. She may be alive, I thought, but just barely. He eyes were almost swollen shut. She looked at us through slits. Her lips started moving when she saw me. In a coarse voice, she said, "Officer Drake, I'm so sorry."

I didn't know how to respond. I'd been put through hell, but I really couldn't put the blame on her. I was glad that Wilson spoke first. He said, "I'm Detective Wilson. I brought Mr. Drake with me because you requested him. I'd like to record this if you don't mind."

"Go ahead, I don't think much more can be done to me," she answered.

Wilson placed a small pocket recorder on a table tray beside her bed switching it on. He said, "This is Detective Kenneth Wilson in the presence of John Drake and…"

"Dr. Karen Williams," said the physician when Wilson hesitated.

"Thank you Dr. Williams," said Wilson continuing. "A Jane Doe brought into University Hospital requested to speak with John Drake concerning an incident at the Double H Lounge."

Wilson went through the dates of the shooting, when Janice was admitted to the hospital and all the usual documentation before he started asking questions. He spoke directly to the woman asking, "What is you legal name and where do you live?"

Without hesitation she said, "Janice Eberstark. I live at 4313 Highview Street."

"Why have you asked us to come and speak with you?" Wilson asked.

"I want to tell Officer Drake what happened," she answered.

"Please call me John. I'm no longer a police officer," I interrupted.

She looked at me before speaking. I sincerely believe there was sorrow and regret on the misshapen face. Tears formed in her eyes as she said, "OK, John didn't kill Frank. My husband, Claus did."

The room fell totally silent except for the beeping of the machines as everybody stared at me. I couldn't believe what I just heard. I must have started to faint because I felt the doctor place her hands on my shoulders. I vaguely remember her telling me to lower my head between my knees. In one single statement, a woman I didn't know, a woman of an ill past, a woman who owed me nothing, proved my innocence."

As my senses came back to me, I struggled to sit up. Wilson's jaw was still dropped. He was as surprised and shocked as I was. Janice didn't wait for Wilson to ask another question. She continued as soon as she saw I had regained my equilibrium, "Frank loved me. He was going to leave his wife. I was going to leave Claus. We were going to make a fresh start, together."

The woman paused for a moment struggling to catch her breath fighting back her emotions, "I made a mistake. I told one of the girls about our plans. Her name's Tammy. She told Claus. He was working the bar that night. It was OK for me to turn tricks, but It wasn't OK for me to leave him. I was his source of income. He went into a rage. He slipped out the back door and up the alley when Frank and John went outside. He killed Frank. He told me he shot Frank, and he'd kill me if I said anything."

"You're speaking of Officer Frank Glass?" asked Wilson for clarification.

"Yes," she answered, her voice becoming coarser. "Claus hid in the alley. It's not lighted. Nobody could see him. He thought Officer Drake, I mean John, might know about us and figure out what happened. The bartender, Brent, called Claus when John came back. Frank tried to kill him too."

"What type of gun did he use?" Wilson asked.

"I don't know exactly what it is. It's like the guns cowboys use. Not the flat guns that police carry. He keeps it in our bedroom. He made a compartment under the floor boards. There's a rug over it with a chest on the rug. I'm so sorry…"

"Is he the one who hurt you?" Wilson probed.

"Claus is a member of the Aryan Brotherhood," she answered clearly showing fatigue. "They run several bars which *their* girls work out of. Wives are shared by the brothers. When a member gets tired of his wife, he turns her into a whore working in the bars. Claus wanted money. He wouldn't let me stop working. I dyed my hair to change my look. He put me to work in one of their other bars."

"John and the black sergeant came to where I was working. Claus wanted to know what I'd told them. He took me back to our house. He wouldn't believe I hadn't said anything. He whipped me with his belt. Then he started beating me with his fists. When I fell to the floor, he started kicking me in the head. I don't remember anything else. I woke up here. It hurt so bad…" she said choking out the words between sobs.

"I think that's enough for now," Dr. Williams said getting to her feet indicating the interview was over.

We followed the doctor to the nurse's station which was out of sight of the woman's room. The nurses sitting at the station were watching us. Wilson asked the doctor for a private place to speak. She motioned with her head for us to follow. We went outside ICU into the hall, where she said, "I don't have an office in the hospital. I could take you to the doctor's lounge, but this is actually more private."

Wilson looked both ways in the hall. Nobody was paying any attention to us. In a low voice, he said, "What you just heard is very confidential. Would you please not repeat anything to anybody? If this information reaches the wrong people before I can do anything about it, she could be put in harm's way. This man is extremely dangerous. He tried to kill her once. If he knew she was talking to the police, he'd try to get to her here."

"Doctors are very good about not repeating what patients say," she replied. "I don't know, in this instance, if it falls under the patient doctor confidentiality rule. Besides, I tend to believe it could put not only her but the staff in harm's way. If somebody asks, I'll tell them it was a follow up visit. She couldn't help you."

"Thank you," a relieved Wilson said. "I'm going back to type up an affidavit of what she said. I'd like to come back for her signature. Would you be opposed to witnessing it?"

"If she gives me verbal permission in front of you, I have no problems witnessing it," stated the doctor with what I thought of as anger flashing across her face. "It takes an animal to do what he did to her. Everybody'll be safer with him off the streets."

Before leaving, Wilson gave the doctor a business card instructing her to call him if she observed anybody unusual hanging around ICU. Neither of us spoke until we got to his car. As Wilson pulled out of the hospital lot, he gave a low whistle before speaking, "Damn! She gave enough that you'll never be convicted. It should be enough to convict her husband. He admitted to her that he shot Frank."

"The bartender must know about it," I said.

"He'd deny knowing anything," Wilson argued. "When I get the affidavit signed, I'm going straight to a judge to get a search warrant signed. The gun's a key part. If I find the gun, then I'll have enough to charge him with murder and make it stick. We didn't find shell casings because it was a revolver. We have testimony from a witness, motive and a weapon. Hopefully, Claus will be at the house. I'll take him into custody on the spot."

"If the ballistics from the revolver matches the slugs from the telephone pole, I can charge him with attempted murder," Wilson added. "She said he shot at you. I can charge the bartender with conspiracy to commit murder."

A Cheshire cat grin came across Wilson's face, "He's going away. The bartender's an added bonus. Hell's bells, this is turning into a good day! After I've got him booked, I'll personally deliver the papers to the DA's office. I want to see the bastard's face when I tell him he indicted the wrong man. I think I'm going to ruin his day!"

"Wouldn't it be a shame if an unnamed newsman just happened to be in the neighborhood when I arrested the asshole," Wilson said conspiratorially.

If I have nothing else, I have a good memory. She had given her address as 4313 High view Street. I'd been fired; therefore, I wasn't restrained from tipping off Mumford. I wasn't a police officer anymore. He deserved an exclusive. He'd hung in there with me. Besides, it'd give

Bellows and Channel 12 a big case of heartburn for being scooped. Payback's hell!

***

Sarah and I were huddled together on the couch waiting for Mumford's station, Channel 46, to start their news broadcast. Mumford had called earlier simply saying we'd find it interesting and shouldn't miss it. Earlier in the day, I had called Mumford telling him to stake out the address. He wanted to know why, but I wouldn't tell him. I was returning the compliment.

The Channel 46 news logo flashed on the screen with Mumford's voice saying, "Stay tuned. Suspect arrested for the murder of Officer Frank Glass!"

The picture changed to Mumford sitting at a long desk with the regular 5 o'clock news anchors. The young brunette at the center said, "You've had an exciting day, Mark."

"Yes, I have," Mumford answered excitedly. "Today police arrested a suspect, Claus Eberstark, charging him with the murder of Officer Frank Glass at the Double H Lounge. The following clip shows Eberstark being led from his house to a police car."

The picture showed a large man with his hands handcuffed behind his back being led to a marked unit by two uniformed officers. I recognized the man! He was the same man who sat at the table watching us in the Pussy Cat Lounge. His chin was tucked against his chest in an attempt to hide his face. Wilson was behind them carrying a large paper bag. There was obviously something heavy in the bag by the way Wilson carried it. Wilson had found the gun.

The next sequence showed Mumford standing next to Wilson. Mumford was holding a microphone. Mumford asked, "What is the man being arrested for?"

Wilson said in a matter of fact voice, "The suspect is being charged with the murder of Police Officer Frank Glass. Call our information officer at headquarters if you have any other questions."

A frontal picture of Eberstark with a series of numbers underneath his face flashed on the screen behind the newscasters. It was his mug shot from booking. "What about John Drake? Wasn't he charged with reckless homicide for the same incident?" the lady anchor asked.

I'm positive the exchange was preplanned giving Mumford an entry to the next news clip. "Judy, I went to the DA's office to ask if the charges against Drake were going to be dropped. The next clip will answer your question."

The video showed the DA coming past the receptionist in the DA office into their lobby. His suit coat was off with his shirt sleeves rolled to the elbows. It was the iconic picture of a hard working DA. His eyes darted around the room as he walked towards Mumford. The small man clearly didn't expect to see the news team. He didn't extend his hand stopping a good three feet from Mumford. Locking eyes on the reporter, he asked, "May I help you?"

Without hesitation, Mumford fired his first question, "Mr. Durbin, are you aware the police have arrested a suspect for the murder of Officer Frank Glass?"

The DA's face answered Mumford's question before he opened his mouth to answer. The DA's eyes widened, and his head jerked back as if slapped. "No," he stammered.

Mumford didn't give him time to recover asking, "How will this affect the charges your office put against John Drake? Will they be dropped?"

I had to admit, the DA was quick on his feet, he quickly responded, "I haven't been informed about this development. I'll have to look into it. After I examine the relevant information, I'll make a decision. A statement will be issued. Thank you for bringing this to my attention."

The DA didn't give Mumford a chance to ask another question. He spun on his heels quickly walking down a hall towards his office. The screen returned to Channel 46's news room. Mumford said, "Judy, in fairness, the DA was not aware of the new development in the Double H Lounge shooting. However, I called his office before our broadcast started, and a statement hasn't been issued at this time."

Mumford picked up a stack of papers as the camera panned back to the anchor newscasters. Judy said, "Mark, this is an interesting turn of events."

"Yes indeed," he answered with the corner of his lips turning upwards.

Sarah and I danced around the room hugging each other in celebration. I wasn't going to jail! We called my folks and Sarah's mother. They were as relieved as we were. Then the telephone started ringing. Thank God for caller ID. The reporters were burning up our line. It never stopped ringing. When one reporter gave up, another reporter called. Finally, I turned the phone's ringer off. How did they all manage to get our telephone number? Did they pass our number around? It was supposed to be unlisted.

Our celebration was again interrupted by a loud knocking on our front door. My first thought was it was a damn reporter! "Don't answer the door," I said too loudly!

"I'll look out the window to see who it is," Sarah answered.

Sarah barely drew back the curtain by the door peeping out. Without speaking, she quickly moved to the door unlocking it. She flung it open leaping out the door. When I ran to the door, I saw Ken Wilson wrapped up in Sarah's arms. His face was lighted with a large grin. I waited for Sarah to unwrap herself before motioning Wilson into the house. As he entered, I couldn't help myself. I gave him a big hug also.

Wilson chuckled before saying, "I wanted to come by and see if you'd heard the news. Apparently you have!"

"Ken, I owe you big time," I blurted!

"No, I was doing my job. It was odd that Mumford was hanging around when I arrested Eberstark," Wilson said giving me a wink.

"Didn't cause you any trouble, did it?" I asked.

"No, it was a good arrest. It made the department look good. I can't say the same about the DA's office," he answered still smiling.

Wilson pulled a folded newspaper style magazine out of his side jacket pocket. Dramatically unfolding it, he handed the magazine to me. It was what I classified as a scandal rag. One of the national ones sold in super markets. On the front page was the picture of our mayor in the compromising position with the teen. The teen's face was blurred beyond recognition, but the headlines screamed: Mayor caught in sex scandal!

Wilson laughed at the expression on my face. Sarah moved beside me scanning the magazine. "They'll get their ass sued off," she commented.

"Not if it's true," he rebutted, pausing to collect his thoughts. "Now that it's in the open, the Crimes against Children Unit will have to investigate. It's the law."

143

I never gave much thought about the future until the chain of events unfolded due to the murder of Frank. The sun hadn't pierced the night's veil when I woke. I slipped out of bed being careful not to wake Sarah. I fumbled in the dark eventually finding my jogging shorts and shoes. It felt good to be on the sidewalk hearing my steps as I ran. I was free. Free to run anywhere I desired. I felt like a thoroughbred horse as my breath formed puffs of steam in the cool crisp air.

Freedom was something I had taken for granted which brought my thought back to the future. I decided that nobody knew the future. A person driving home from work who was killed by a drunk driver didn't plan on being killed. Heart attacks took out people whom loved ones would never see again, at least in this life. I was going to live each day to the fullest. I wasn't going to forget the simple things such as saying I love you to Sarah and Amy.

I sprinted around the corner finishing my run. As I walked the block cooling down, white wisps of steam rose from my shoulders. The kitchen light was on in our house. I saw a shadow move across the curtains. Sarah was fixing coffee. I picked the paper up off the front porch tucking it under my arm before unlocking the front door. The aroma of coffee brewing floated in the air. Sarah came out of the kitchen with a mug of coffee handing it to me.

"You're up early," she said stifling a yawn.

"Been a long time since I've felt this good. I love you," I said giving her a peak on the cheek.

"I know. I've always known," she answered smiling. "Come on you big galoot. I'll fix breakfast while you read the paper."

I sipped the coffee as I followed. It was perfect. It just the way I like it – strong. As I said before, we take the simple things for granted. I unrolled the newspaper as I sat at the table. The front page, above the fold, was about Eberstark's arrest. I scanned the article. There was nothing I didn't already know. The article did make a point of reporting the DA hadn't issued a statement concerning the charge against me. Give the newspaper an attaboy.

Surprise, surprise! The editorial section had a piece blasting the DA. In a nutshell, it questioned why I was indicted when a murderer was running loose. Did the police and DA need to investigate the investigation? Good play on words. Then it questioned why the charge against me hadn't been dismissed. How could two people have shot the man if he had been shot only once? Another attaboy for the newspaper. Heavens forbid! I was starting to like the press. I guess all reporters can't be bad, or they like kicking whoever's down. You couldn't accuse them of being prejudice.

Buried in the second section of the newspaper, below the fold, was a small article on Jacob Bellows. According to the article he was arrested for DUI, driving on a suspended license and resisting arrest. A Sgt. William Hickman observed him driving erratically on the expressway at 2:00 A.M. Bellows blew a 0.19 on the alcohol breathalyzer. It stated Bellows fought with the officer refusing to be arrested. An interesting side note stated Bellows refused medical treatment before being taken to jail.

I'd have to talk to the sarge to get the scoop on what happened. Reading between the lines, Bellows got squirrely with the sarge and got his ass kicked. A mean drunk with an attitude can be hard to handle and dangerous. I made a mental note to give Hickman an attaboy. Maybe I should read the paper more often. It wasn't always bad news. Of course, it's according to your perspective.

From the DA's and Bellows' perspectives, it wasn't good news. It's hard to have sympathy for somebody who wanted to put you in jail for a crime you didn't commit. Bellows would get a taste of what he wanted for me. I recalled it wasn't the first time he was arrested for DUI. That's why he had a suspended license. With a good lawyer, I doubted he'd get any time. Most likely, he'd get another probated sentence.

The DA was a different matter. I don't know if he broke any laws by the way he presented the facts. I vaguely recall a DA being prosecuted for omitting a few selective facts. I chuckled, thinking of another play on words, prosecutor being prosecuted. The newspaper had a good point. Both of us couldn't have shot Frank.

Whether the DA had caved to political pressure or had sacrificed me for political ambitions, I didn't know or care. This wasn't going to help his re-election campaign. I figured he'd issue a statement today dropping the charge. Then, he'd crawl back into his hole and pull it shut. It's called weathering the storm. How many politicians have been re-elected after caught in a scandalous act? Politically, bad PR is not necessarily a bad thing. If enough time passes, voters forget the gaff but remember the name on Election Day.

I set the paper aside when Sarah put a plate of scrambled eggs, bacon and toast in front of me. She had two pieces of toast and coffee. She preferred a light breakfast. I told her about the newspaper articles. I admit that I was somewhat full of myself, but Sarah brought me back to reality, "John, you... We have to move on with our lives. Being angry is a normal reaction. But, if you hold a grudge or hate, it becomes a cancer destroying you from within. Do want to become like Bellows?"

That was a sobering thought. Anger was a slippery slope. If I let it slip into hate, then I became a mirror reflection of what caused the anger. She was a step ahead of me, again. Another thought popped into my mind. In the academy, an instructor said, "You're job is to enforce the law, not to judge people after they're arrested. A crime may offend your sense of morality, but you are an extension of the executive branch which is sworn to uphold the laws passed by the people's representatives. Present the facts and let the court judge the offender.

In a sense, Sarah was saying the same thing. I didn't have to hold a grudge. Both individuals would be judged by the public and by their peers. Justifiable anger is proper. It motivates an individual to correct the wrong. Hate destroys the individual. I nodded at Sarah and smiled. We moved on to more important subjects, like what I needed to get for supper.

CHAPTER 15

Today was Amy day. I volunteered to keep Amy giving my Mom a break. I got the feeling during the phone conversation that Mom wasn't too thrilled with the idea. I think she insinuated men were incompetent with toddlers. My ego was bruised. Actually, Mom was pleased to have a day off. She mentioned dragging Dad out the door to go shopping. I'm sure I'll hear from him later. I should have forewarned him so he could have had an excuse or hid.

After breakfast, I bathed Amy. I thought about how many baths Amy took. It's a wonder she didn't look like a prune. As I watched her splash, I reflected on how close I had come to losing this part of my life. I reminded myself of what Sarah had said. I had to move ahead with life. Amy stretched her arms upwards. Her wiggly little fingers signaled she wanted to be held. I was blessed.

Mom may have been correct about men being incompetent with toddlers. Have you tried to diaper a toddler who doesn't want a diaper? I did get the diaper on Amy, sort of. The one piece jumpsuit was an interesting experience. It was an epic battle of wills. A truce was negotiated. I put Amy in her highchair with some Cheerios to push around the tray.

Sarah checked in to see how I was doing. What is it with women? I can hold my own with Amy, most of the time. The rest of the morning was spent doing chores, simple things like washing clothes, leaving them in the dryer too long and folding the wrinkled clothes. After lunch, I put Amy in the crib for a nap. I remembered to call Sgt. Hickman.

I called him on his personal cell phone. I didn't want the possibility of anybody listening in on the conversation. Hickman said he'd call me back. He was going to a location for privacy because cops are nosey and will eavesdrop on a conversation. It was only a few seconds before my phone rang. "Hey John, I'm glad you called. I was thinking about calling you," he said.

"I saw the article in the paper about Bellow's arrest," indicating I was curious.

There was a lag before he answered which I took as he was making up his mind whether to broach the subject or not. "It was karma," he chuckled. "I had worked over and was heading home. Man, he was all over the road. I'm surprised he hadn't wrecked. Anyway, it took a long time for him to pull over once I lit him up. I had no problem giving him the breathalyzer. When I told him he was under arrest, he told me I couldn't arrest him because he was a reporter. It went downhill from there. It wasn't much of a scuffle though. He had a few scrapes to the face from the pavement."

"That's not the reason I wanted to speak with you," he added. "The ballistics results on Eberstark's pistol match the bullet fired at you. Detective Wilson has charged Eberstark with attempted murder. It validates his wife's testimony. Wilson's hunting the bartender who tipped Eberstark you were at the bar. Wilson will charge him with attempted murder. He helped Eberstark try to kill you by making the phone call."

Hickman continued without giving me time to ask any questions, "I spoke with the president of the FOP. They believe the DA will drop the charge against you today. They're petitioning the merit board to have you reinstated. They gave the merit board a solid list of officers who were disciplined for working off duty jobs without permission. None of the officers were fired. Fellows has notified the board that he'll file a lawsuit on your behalf if you're not reinstated with back pay."

Over the phone, I heard a loud knocking. Hickman said, "Got to go John. I'll call you back later."

Amy was still complaining about taking a nap. I poked my head into her room just enough to see if she had her eyes closed. Police are good at surveillance. As a responsible adult, I felt it was my duty to set a good example for Amy, so I sacked out on the couch to take a nap. Why is it that when you get comfortable drifting off with pleasant dreams, somebody has to disturb you? It must be some kind of axiom.

The doorbell rang followed by knocking at the door. Not thinking about who was on the other side, I swung the door open. I caught Wilson with his arm raised to knock again. He was dressed in a blue blazer, grey slacks and a natty red regimental tie. His badge and gun were barely showing on his belt. "I need to speak with you," he said.

I nodded to him to come in as I said, "I spoke with Sergeant Hickman today. He brought me up to date on the case."

Amy was starting to cry, so I brought her to the living room. I put her on the floor with a few toys. Wilson had settled on the couch. "The reason I came by was to talk to you about Ali Johnson," said Wilson. "Somebody put the fear of God in him. He set up a meeting with me this morning as far away from the hood as possible at a yuppie coffee shop in WASP country. He's willing to turn state evidence if he's given a new identity and placed in the federal witness protection program."

He had my full attention. I asked, "What did he say about the shooting?"

"I'll get to that in a second," Wilson answered. "Johnson has a cut on the side of his neck close to the jugular. He claims, and I quote, 'some white cracker motherfucker dressed like a ninja been stalking me. Put a knife to my fuckin' throat. Told me if I didn't turn myself in and come clean, the next time he'd finished the job. Said he'd leave me a reminder and cut my neck. The dude's crazy.' He said he couldn't identify the man. I think it'd be wise if the ninja disappeared."

We locked eyes. I knew what Wilson was saying without him saying it. It's a man thing. Men can read another man's body language better than women can. The reverse is true for women. Sarah has told me another woman was making a pass at me when I thought she was being friendly. Both of us thought of my Dad. I remembered seeing Dad dressed in black fatigues coming home from being out all night.

"I have no idea who his assailant could be," I said playing along. "But, I think I'll mention it to Dad and get his assessment."

"I think it'd be a good idea," said Wilson in a tone which stated that he'd let it slide this time, but it wouldn't be tolerated again.

Both of us knew a non verbal agreement had been reached. Clearing my throat signaling a new topic, I asked, "What else did he say?"

"For your ears only John. Nobody's to be told. Not Sarah, not your Dad, not Hickman. Agreed?" he asked.

"OK," I answered.

"Treece and Johnson were going to the bar to pick up a shipment of cocaine. We were wrong about the pecking order. Treece was the muscle. Johnson was the money man. They spotted Glass' badge jumping to the conclusion they were set up. They hadn't spotted you because you were lagging behind Glass at an angle. Treece pulled his gun. There was no doubt in Johnson's mind that Treece was going to shoot his way out. Johnson says he wasn't armed, if you can believe him. He said he ran because he had five thousand in cash on him. He's smart enough to know it'd be confiscated if he were arrested."

"Did he say anything about the drive by shooting at my house? How'd they know where I lived?" I asked.

Wilson looked angry as he answered, "Johnson said he wasn't involved in the drive by although he admits his peeps did it. He said it was a matter of respect. You didn't show any respect for his peeps. Pure bullshit! They figured out where you lived by watching the news. One of the stations did an intro in front of your subdivision. The subdivision's sign was used as the backdrop. Your house was on other news clips. It didn't take a rocket scientist to put two and two together to get the answer."

"I've contacted an agent I know in the FBI," he continued. "They're interested. The FBI, ATFA and DEA have a joint task force tracking the skinheads. The Aryans are doing business with the Mexican mafia, La Eme, smuggling drugs and arms. Johnson's testimony will give enough credence to get a warrant to raid the skinhead's compound."

Wilson bent over tussling Amy's hair before standing. His mission was accomplished. I'd have to find a way to approach Dad about the matter without accusing. After he left, I channel surfed settling on a local news program. Men are experts at channel surfing. I played with Amy on the floor until a segment caught my attention. The DA was giving a statement. He held a single piece of paper and read directly from it without looking into the camera.

He read, "With the new evidence uncovered by the police pertaining to the murder of Officer Frank Glass, the District Attorney's Office is withdrawing the charge of reckless homicide against former Officer John Drake. The office's objective is to administer justice in behalf of the people. We will vigorously pursue the prosecution of the people charged with the murder of Officer Glass. Thank you. No questions will be entertained."

The news program switched to a different story after a short comment that the station would bring updates on the unfolding investigation about the murder of Officer Glass. Instead of feeling exuberance, I felt anger at being publically and privately humiliated for the political gain of others. A voice interrupted my thoughts. Oddly enough, it sounded like Sarah's voice although I knew she wasn't present.

The voice reminded me that some good things had emerged from this tragedy. I was reunited with my wife. I wouldn't have been with the small child playing at my feet. Dad and I had rebuilt a solid relationship. Hubris. Don't let pride destroy you. There was nothing left to prove. I had been exonerated. The others were responsible for their actions and the consequences of those actions. I needed to get on with my life.

The phone rang. My first inclination was that it was a reporter asking how I felt about the charge being dropped. The caller ID showed it was from Fellows' law offices. When I answered, Fellows said, "I've had some discussion with Channel 12's attorneys. At the present, they're taking the stance that Bellows was supposed to have been off the air when he made the defamatory statement. Because it was a programming error, Bellows and they are not to be held accountable although they did allude to a token settlement without admission of guilt to make it go away.

"John, I believe they know they're on tenuous ground; otherwise, there wouldn't have been a token offer. They're fishing to see how determined we are. I think we should file suit. That'll show them we're serious."

I agreed to let Fellows file a lawsuit against Channel 12 and Bellows, personally. I didn't care if I got any money from the lawsuit. I wanted the news people to know they were accountable for their actions just like they wanted me held accountable. How did they feel having the positions reversed? I reminded myself that reporters were just people. There are more good people than bad. Channel 12 had hired a bad apple. They should have done their homework better before hiring Bellows.

***

151

I called Dad asking him to come to our house and explaining I wanted to update him. He didn't question why I couldn't tell him over the phone. Perhaps he didn't trust the security of a phone line? Probably, he wanted to visit or update me on his activities, but I doubted it was the latter. I wanted to speak with him in person about the ninja doing a disappearing act. You can't read a person's reaction over a telephone. I wanted to see his reaction to the ninja episode to give me a clue to if he were the masked avenger or vigilante depending on your viewpoint.

Amy had fallen asleep on the carpet. Not wanting to wake her, I covered her with a small blanket. I kept the front door open watching out the kitchen windows as I made a pot of coffee. I intercepted Dad at the front door placing a finger over my lips for silence. We quietly settled in the kitchen with me taking a seat so I could keep an eye on Amy.

Once I poured the coffee, I relayed everything that had happened today with the exception of the ninja and Johnson. Dad dutifully listened without commenting. Acting as if I had forgotten, I said, "Oh, Wilson said the gang member, Ali Johnson, contacted him. Johnson claims somebody's threatening his life. He's convinced enough to turn state evidence."

"And?" Dad asked as if it was all new to him.

"Wilson doesn't want Johnson injured. He's too valuable of a source," I answered in a voice that I hoped wouldn't be taken as accusatory. "He said Johnson described the man as a ninja and couldn't identify him."

There was a flash in Dad's eyes which I couldn't interpret. In a voice that related amusement rather than guilt, he said, "I think that Johnson character's been watching too many ninja movies. I can't recall seeing a ninja around these parts lately. Anyway, I'd suspect if the ninja completed his mission, he'd be on his way back to Japan. Don't think Johnson will see him again."

Though he didn't outright admit to being the man dressed in black, I felt the ninja had completed his tour of duty and wouldn't reappear. There were many questions I wanted to ask but knew better than to go there. I had accomplished what Wilson had demanded. A potential wildfire smothered before it blazed out of control.

***

I liked jogging in the early morning. It gave me a semblance of a routine and schedule. More importantly, it was my time of contemplation. I enjoyed the cool crisp air and the lonely sounds of my footsteps on the pavement as I let my mind wander. I was thinking about the future, now that I had one again. If I were reinstated on the police department, did I really want to go back? Dad had a good life working construction, a normal schedule, time home with the family and decent money.

As I saw my house coming within sight, I decided I'd talk about it with Dad. I'd come to appreciate his insight if not his "different" approach to situations. There's something to be said for experience. I retrieved the newspaper out of the paper box unfolding it as I walked to the front door. The headline immediately grabbed my attention: "MAYOR MICHAELS ARRESTED IN SEX SCANDAL!" Not bothering to make coffee, I sat at the kitchen table. The article read:

Mayor Michaels was arrested late Wednesday evening charged with sexual abuse in the first degree. After a compromising photograph of the mayor was published, a woman who claimed to be the mother of the teen in the photograph contacted the Crimes against Children Unit. Undisclosed sources state that she recognized her son in the photograph while standing in a checkout line at a grocery store.

The mother turned over to the police a shirt she claims her son was wearing in the photograph. She stated that she hadn't laundered the shirt. The shirt has stains on it which she thought to be bodily fluid. Samples have been sent to the lab for DNA analysis. She brought her son to the police to be interviewed.

The teenager confirmed he was paid by Michaels for sex. The teenager gave the police a list of other youths he claims had sex with Michaels for money. The police are continuing to investigate. The police would not release the names of the mother and son stating they are held confidential by law.

"Police Chief Hardesty would not comment on the arrest because it was an ongoing investigation. The mayor's office has not released a statement as of the time this article went to press. The DA Office

was past normal business hours when the arrest was made. Calls to the DA's home were not returned to the paper. Continued on back page,
section A.

Sarah came into the kitchen dressed in pajamas with a bathrobe hanging open. I was speechless thrusting the newspaper into her hands. Her eyes widened as she read. When she finished, she handed the newspaper back to me saying, "Michaels won't have to be worried about being re-elected. His biggest concern will be staying out of prison!"

"Child molesters fare worst than police officers in prison," I responded. "If he's convicted, he'll be lucky to survive."

"He didn't care if you survived," Sarah said angrily pausing to think. "This'll bring down his whole administration. Even the police chief will be tainted. I think the DA is going to get splattered by this scandal. I bet he wishes he never stood in front of the cameras with those two."

***

I took Amy to my Mother to babysit because I had to go to Fellows' office to sign some papers. The apple doesn't fall far from the tree. Dad was sitting at the kitchen table reading the newspaper. "Interesting development, isn't it John?" he asked with a wink.

"What do you think will come out of it?" I asked.

"He'll serve some time," he answered. "How much? I reckon it depends upon the judge. His political career is finished though."

Mom came into the kitchen, and Amy stretched her arms towards Mom squealing, "Mamaw!"

I transferred Amy to Mom, got a cup of coffee and sat at the table across from Dad. Mom disappeared with Amy. Dad could tell I had something on my mind. He folded the paper setting it to the side giving me his full attention. "I've been thinking about what I want to do in the future," I said. "I'm not too sure if I want to go back on the police force even if I'm reinstated. There'll always be a blemish on my record. Some officers will have a lingering doubt."

"I can see where you're coming from," he answered and continued without waiting for a response. "But, the real question you have to ask yourself is, do you like being a police officer? If the answer is yes, then go back. I'd suggest not making a snap decision. You can resign if the situation is intolerable. More importantly, discuss it with Sarah. It's a joint decision that affects both of your lives."

***

I mulled Dad's advice over as I drove to Fellows' law office. I liked being a cop, but Dad was right about it being a joint decision. I'd talk to Sarah tonight. I wasn't the only one who had been through an emotional trauma. She owned a piece of this decision if I was reinstated.

I put the conversation that I had with Dad and the discussion with Sarah out of my mind as I went into Fellows' law offices. It would be moot if the termination held. I realized that I was still in a state of limbo. I was not in as a precarious position as going to jail, but my financial position was insecure. I was still unemployed.

Without having to wait, I was ushered to Fellows' private office. Fellows was sitting behind his desk which was stacked with files. A blue pinstriped suit coat was hanging from a clothes tree in the corner. He wore a silk shirt with French cuffs accentuated with black onyx cuff links. A satin yellow tie was fastened to his neck by a Winsor knot. Peering over his gold framed reading glasses, Fellows said, "Make yourself comfortable John. We have a lot to cover."

Fellows filled a china cup with coffee for me before continuing, "Channel 12's attorney contacted me this morning. Their token offer is a little more than what I'd consider token. They've offered $250,000 dollars if you're willing to sign an agreement not to pursue this matter with a non disclosure clause about the settlement. As far as Bellows, they're leaving him flapping in the wind."

I was unable to speak for a moment before sputtering, "What do you recommend."

Fellows did not reply immediately. He thoughtfully looked at the files on his desk before answering, "Potentially, it's worth a lot more than they're offering, but if you take this case to trial, there is always the possibility you could lose. I'd advise settling. I wouldn't pursue litigation against Bellows. I don't believe he has any resources. Of course, I'll do whatever you decide."

I didn't have a vendetta against Channel 12. I'm sure it stung their pride having to make a monetary settlement. As far as Bellows was concerned, I wasn't going to hold a grudge against him. I was going to do what Sarah had said. I was going to get on with my life and not live in the past.

"I'm going to follow you advice," I said. "Please take their offer."

Fellows seemed pleased as he said, "The merit board is meeting today to consider a petition filed by the F.O.P. I'm not at liberty to discuss the source of my information, but from my understanding you'll be reinstated with full back pay. You'll receive written notification tomorrow, and I suspect a phone call."

I don't know how to express the emotions that I felt. I couldn't stop the tears forming at the corner of my eyes spilling down my cheeks. The horror that started a few days ago was coming to an end. Fellows didn't say anything. He took an embroidered handkerchief from the top drawer of his desk handing it to me. Fellows was smiling. It wasn't a smug smile, but a smile of satisfaction.

***

It seemed I was always bumping into Mumford. I was walking to my car thinking about the meeting with Fellows. A car horn broke my train of thought. I looked in the direction of the noise. It was Mumford pulling his car next to the curb. He was waving at me. The passenger's side of the car was facing the curb with its window down. I stooped and leaned on the door to speak to him. Mumford turned off the engine and unbuckled his seat belt. Leaning across the car, he offered his hand.

As we shook hands, he said, "I'm pleased that everything worked out for you. Let's stay in touch. Remember, I'm on your side. It helps to have a reporter who understands the challenges the police face."

On the passenger seat was a stack of comic books in protective covers. The comic book on top of the stack was "The Guardian of Justice". It was issue 614. Mumford saw me staring at the top copy. He explained, "I collect comic books. It's a passion I've had since childhood. Super heroes fighting crime and injustices. If only it were true."

My mind shifted into high gear. I started to connect the dots. Mumford was in the business of knowing what was happening. He was an

156

investigative reporter. He would know the rumors circulating about politicians. He was trained to take photographs. It all added up! I decided that some subjects were better not to be discussed. I reached into the car and turned the comic book face down. It was my way of saying the subject was closed.

I thanked him for his support, and then we talked a short time. Nothing important was brought up. I'd classify it as idle chatter. I thought about Mumford as I walked to my car. Were the comic book characters a role model for him when he was a child? Did he see himself as avenging injustice? You can never know how another person perceives reality.

EPILOGUE

I was standing in front of the mirror examining the man dressed in the dark blue uniform. The dark colors of the uniform represented authority in people's eyes. The fly line was perfectly straight with the gun belt buckle directly over it. The polished badge glistened in the mirror. The uniform didn't feel strange. It felt comfortable.

I saw a blonde woman walk behind me. Her arms slid around my waist firmly hugging me. "How do I look?" I asked.

"Good," she answered. "The uniform doesn't make the man. The man makes the uniform. John, you're a good man. You're my man. Always."

"Always," I repeated as I firmly kissed Sarah on the lips before leaving to participate in the future unfolding.

Driving to the station, I reflected upon the last few days. What did I learn? No person knows his future. When we think we have it planned, the fates delight in throwing our life into turmoil as Clotho spins the thread of life. We could be stripped of all possessions through no fault of our own.

All things, except for the essence of life, are just material things. Things can be replaced. The spirit that dwells in the flesh cannot be replaced once it flees. The true joy in life is experienced when kindred souls join forging a union. The union of souls is what allows us to survive. I am part of that union.

NOVELS BY D.W. HARDIN

Hidden and Imminent Dangers (Pandemic)

A Time To Lie (John Drake Crime Novel)

Wooing The Fates (Det. John Drake Crime Novel)

The Black Widow Does Not Cry (Det. John Drake Crime Novel)

Refuge (Science Fiction)

Here's an excerpt from *Hidden and Imminent Dangers*.
It's about a pandemic of biblical scale. If you enjoy
apocalyptical characters hidden in a story,
you'll love *Hidden and Imminent Dangers*!

PROLOGUE

Billy could hear the woman doctor speaking to his parents. His father was crying loudly while his mother sobbed. When the doctor told his parents he wouldn't live, he wanted to shout she was wrong—he didn't want to die! But he was so tired and weak that his body couldn't respond to his mind's commands. His mind shouted *PLEASE HELP ME!* The doctor was leaning over him handling the tube running down his throat. The rhythmic rush of air down his throat stopped as he heard a snipping sound. As the tube slid out of his throat, he felt as if he were suffocating. After taking three deep breaths, his next breaths were very shallow. His breathing became cyclic. A few deep breaths, then shallow breathing until the body cried for more oxygen.

Instinct told him death was approaching. Flashes of his life came into his mind. He was reviewing his life as if he were a spectator watching a movie. He saw himself as a small child in the third grade. He was in geography class paging through a *National Geographic* amazed at all the different world cultures presented in vivid pictures. Strange tribes with bones pushed through their noses. Topless women whose lips protruded from discs somehow used to disfigure them. Asians dressed in flowing kimonos. Things he always wanted to experience.

Billy had barely graduated from high school. His father had a ninth-grade education and hadn't seen any need for his son to be educated. His father had farm chores keeping Billy busy until dark on school nights. After he finished the chores, he was too tired and dirty to care about homework. His father worked him like a man without time to play like his classmates. Without realizing it, Billy had drifted into being a loner. Yet he kept his dreams of traveling the world, dreaming of what it would be like to be Marco Polo or Stanley Livingston.

He remembered the liquid blue eyes of Peggy. She lived on an adjoining farm and was trapped just like him. Although he was two years older than her, they had a strong mutual attraction both mentally and physically. They would meet in a wooded area farthest away from both farm houses as often as possible. Peggy said she was joining the navy as soon as she graduated from high school. That was the only way she could escape. Billy had dreamed about visiting exotic ports as a sailor. At the time, he didn't know if he had the courage to face his father and enlist. His father depended so heavily on his help. He didn't know if his father could manage the farm by himself. Still, he had been paid a meagerly sum. He never had enough money to even buy a nice car.

Billy saw himself and Peggy lying under the shade of a large maple tree concealed by high grass. He could feel her warm breasts pushed against his chest with one of her legs covering his manhood. Both were wet with perspiration from their inept lovemaking. It had been the first time for both of them. She had cried out in pain and then in pleasure as he had taken her. A light smear of blood on the inside of her thigh had scared him. He had wanted her so bad, straining to enter her and fearing he had somehow internally hurt her. Calming his fears, she lay against him lightly kissing his lips before explaining it was natural for a woman to bleed a little the first time.

Billy never saw Peggy again. The next day, her father came to see his father. Both men huddled together at a distance they considered to be out of earshot. Billy did hear Peggy's father say something about his wife finding blood on clothes, and he didn't want Billy around her. Afterwards his father bluntly told him to stay away from Peggy. For weeks Billy hung around their meeting spot, but he never saw her. Peggy was the only friend he had ever known.

Billy had not told his parents he had seen a navy recruiter and had committed to join. He was to leave for boot camp the first week in January. He just hadn't worked up the courage to tell them. The recruiter said Billy would have the opportunity to travel the world with time off at ports to see the sights. At last! He would fulfill his dreams! Perhaps he would get to

162

see Peggy again once she enlisted. Maybe they could be on the same ship together! Dreams! What was life without dreams?

A cooling sensation flowed through his veins with all pain creeping away. He was having trouble thinking but didn't care. Everything began to fade into a light fog. It felt so good! He knew that his breathing had stopped, but it didn't matter. He heard a final gurgling sound before everything became black. Billy greeted death.

Made in the USA
Columbia, SC
30 May 2023

17180213R00095